THE CHILL FACTOR

Richard Falkirk was a pseudonym of Derek Lambert, who was born in 1929. He served in the RAF for two and a half years and then worked as a journalist for local newspapers, becoming a foreign correspondent on the *Daily Mirror* and then the *Daily Express*, travelling the world to dangerous locations that later inspired his books. His first novel, *Angels in the Snow* (1969), was based on first-hand knowledge from a year's assignment to Moscow and entailed him smuggling the manuscript out of the country in a wheelchair. From journeying up the Himalayas in a jeep to being shot at in Israel, his experiences informed his authentic tales of espionage and adventure that helped turn him into a bestselling author of more than 30 thrillers. Derek's last book, *Spanish Lessons*, is an affectionate and often hilarious account of giving up life as a globe-trotting journalist to settle down to life in rural Spain with his wife Diane, where he died in 2001 at the age of 71.

The Chill Factor

Suspense and Espionage in Cold War Iceland

DEREK LAMBERT

writing as
RICHARD FALKIRK

HarperCollins*Publishers*

HarperCollins*Publishers*
1 London Bridge Street
London SE1 9GF
www.harpercollins.co.uk

50th Anniversary edition 2021
1

First published in Great Britain by Michael Joseph Ltd
in association with Arlington Books 1971

Introduction © Ragnar Jónasson 2021

Richard Falkirk asserts the moral right
to be identified as the author of this work.

A catalogue record for this book
is available from the British Library

ISBN 978-0-00-843387-1

Typeset in Meridien by
Palimpsest Book Production Ltd, Falkirk, Stirlingshire

Printed and bound in Great Britain by
CPI Group (UK) Ltd, Croydon CR0 4YY

MIX
Paper from
responsible sources
FSC™ C007454

This book is produced from independently certified FSC™ paper
to ensure responsible forest management.

For more information visit: www.harpercollins.co.uk/green

Iceland. In the winter it gets light at 10 a.m. and dark at 2 p.m. There is a daily announcement of the **Chill Factor**, by which the mathematically minded can calculate how quickly they could die from exposure . . .

INTRODUCTION

Glöggt er gests augað.

This Icelandic saying came to mind while reading Richard Falkirk's espionage thriller *The Chill Factor*. It means simply that an outside visitor often sees things more clearly than the locals, and is certainly true – more or less – in Falkirk's book.

The Chill Factor was first published in 1971, when crime and thriller fiction was almost unheard of in Iceland. The first Icelandic detective novel is generally considered to have been written in 1926, actually during what is now considered to be the Golden Age of crime fiction. However, there was no such Golden Age in Iceland. Only a handful of other books followed, and there are then no records on any lists of a single crime novel written in Icelandic from 1950 until the early 1970s. From then on books were few and far between, with the proper 'golden age' of the Icelandic crime novel not commencing until 1997, when Arnaldur Indridason published his first book. The reason for the lack of Icelandic thrillers for most of the twentieth century was simple: readers (and indeed writers) felt that Iceland was too small a place in which to set believable murder mysteries.

And so, in 1971, Richard Falkirk was entering largely uncharted territory, writing a contemporary thriller set in Iceland. Interestingly, Desmond Bagley had beaten him to it by a matter of months with his espionage thriller *Running Blind*, published at the end of 1970, and its instant popularity should have been a clue to Falkirk's publishers that they had another potential success on their hands. Falkirk – whose real name was Derek Lambert (1929–2001) – worked as a foreign correspondent for the British press, and he had spent time in Iceland prior to writing the book, as was his modus operandi for many of his novels. His descriptions of people, places and customs are accordingly quite vivid. As one might expect in the heightened world of adventure fiction, some of the statements about the local people are overly exaggerated, and occasionally incorrect, but many would have been instantly recognizable to an Icelandic reader at that time.

Now, fifty years later, much of Falkirk's book evokes an Iceland that few writers were capturing at that time, such as this charming description of Reykjavik in the early 1970s:

'Austurvollur Square was still toytown with the little white Lutheran Cathedral and the Althing – the diminutive Parliament building. In the streets around the square the same bookshops, glossy with Icelandic geography and culture from the time of the sagas to the contemporary Nobel Prize winner Halldor Laxness. Chanting newspaper boys, a policeman in white peaked cap and gloves, teenagers in flared trousers and brown and fawn sweaters, no hoardings, no dogs, all in miniature.'

The Reykjavik that forms the backdrop to this novel, with the US naval air station at nearby Keflavik, is somewhat unknown to me, as the story takes place in the early 1970s before I was born. Keflavik was closed and the

Americans left in 2006. But even though these Cold War icons have passed into history, Richard Falkirk's story transports the reader to this faraway time and place; a Reykjavik smaller and more quiet than the one we know now. This is the Reykjavik my parents knew as a young couple, and funnily enough the Icelandic Gudrun drives a 'baby Fiat', just as they did at the time. And when they got engaged, they went for dinner at the Naust restaurant, which also features in the book.

Even though the Icelandic crime novel hadn't really made an appearance in the 1970s, readers there were still enjoying mysteries and thrillers in translation, with authors such as Alistair MacLean and Agatha Christie proving highly popular. *The Chill Factor* rapidly found its way to Icelandic readers, as it was published in translation within a year, in time for 1972's traditional Icelandic Christmas book flood. In fact, the book made headlines in Iceland, with one of the leading newspapers of the time, *Vísir*, running a prominent piece on the novel in November 1972 with the headline: *An Icelandic stewardess the leading character of a foreign novel.* The publisher also took advantage of the Icelandic connection, advertising the book with the strapline: *A foreign author chooses Iceland as a setting.* The ad goes on to say: 'The leading characters are a British man and an Icelandic stewardess at Icelandair. The novel also features the Russian embassy, the Iceland Defence Force, the Icelandic police, the National Registry, clubs and coffee shops in Reykjavik, and various locations outside of Reykjavik.'

The translator, Bárður Halldórsson, was perhaps more sceptical than his publisher, as his introduction to the Icelandic edition carried a word of warning to Icelandic readers:

'The author of this book . . . travelled around Iceland and acquainted himself well with the situation here, as is clear from the reading of the book. However, some of his statements about Iceland and Icelandairs may be disputable and some readers may take offence, as the story is often quite satirical, even ironic. The author sometimes also gets his facts wrong and makes a few mistakes here and there. I decided not to change that in the translation, as such errors give the novel an air of freshness and foreignness. The author is not writing a work of historical accuracy and he has hardly expected the novel become an immortal work of literature, but in spite of all of that, the author's reflections on Icelanders – their nature and disposition – makes it superior to most thrillers.'

The novel is indeed filled with interesting details about life in Iceland, but as the translator notes, some of the statements need to be taken with a grain of salt, delivered as they are with the characteristic flippancy of a fictional secret agent! He remarks, for example, that the second names in Iceland are so alike that phone numbers are listed under Christian names. The second part is quite true, but the reason is perhaps more complicated. He also mentions that in Iceland the weather can change by the minute, which unfortunately *is* very true. 'You should have come last week for the sunshine,' says Gudrun – a wonderful line, capturing in a subtle way the fact that Icelanders love to talk about the weather, especially the elusive sun.

It is also never too late to do anything in Iceland: 'To drink or make the love. At least not in the summer when we have no night. In the winter it is different – then we sleep.' And following this statement, the character of course offers the protagonist aquavit and a bottle of Black Death – Iceland's signature drink. Falkirk was also aware that beer was not allowed in Iceland (not until 1989, in fact): 'The Government does not allow much alcohol in the beer – they think it will encourage drunkenness.'

One of the appeals of spy thrillers from this era – and of Falkirk in particular – is the presence of dry humour to move the story along, and he spices things up with some very broad generalisations: 'You'll like him. A great drinker, a great joker – like most Icelanders,' is one example. Another is that Icelanders are 'Very friendly, very inquisitive, very tough. They also like to tell you about their dreams.' And yet another is the assertion that sweets are apparently an indulgence shared by many Icelanders.

You can tell the author was a journalist, as he never wastes an opportunity to extract humour from something he has observed. During his visit to Iceland he obviously noticed the tendency of some English-speaking Icelanders to use 'v' instead of 'w' and vice versa:

'But you are alive and that is vonderful.'
'Wery,' I said.

And I think it's safe to say that reading Richard Falkirk's previously forgotten book is truly a *wery vonderful wisit* into the past, all the way back to the toytown of Reykjavik in 1971.

RAGNAR JÓNASSON

Ragnar Jónasson is the award-winning author of the bestselling Dark Iceland *series and the* Hulda Trilogy, *called 'a landmark in modern crime fiction' by* The Times. *His books are published in 27 languages, and his first standalone novel,* The Girl Who Died, *is published in 2021. Ragnar lives in Reykjavik.*

CONTENTS

In a book called *Letters from Iceland* first published in 1937, W. H. Auden replied to a question from Christopher Isherwood. *Question*: 'What about the sex life?' *Answer*: 'Uninhibited.'

1

The Stewardess

At least they warned you. The first club listed for Reykjavik in the guide book was *Alcoholics Anonymous – open daily 1800-1900, tel. 16373*. I didn't recall the need for such an establishment, but I was only twelve when I was last in Iceland.

I asked the stewardess the price of a miniature vodka. 'Too cheap,' she said, discarding cosmetic charm as if her boyfriend were invariably incapacitated by Stolichnaya. That was the second warning.

'I'll have one,' I said.

The smile reappeared, as sincere as a TV advertisement. 'Very well, sir.' Slight American accent, hair blonde and slithery, body slender in red skirt and blue blouse representing the fire and ice of Iceland.

I looked out of the window of the Icelandair Saga Jet, a Boeing 727. Pastures of grey cloud were far below; it never seemed to be proper to inspect clouds from above – it made Nature appear vulnerable.

I returned to *Iceland in a Nutshell*. On the cover Hekla was erupting in the snow in a great convoluted brain of smoke. Inside the covers were the desolate grandeurs of the Iceland I remembered. Waterfalls, glaciers, red tongues of lava tasting the cold; clean skies, geysers and towns with green and red roofs like playing cards. Civilisation in the Ice Age melted a little by the Gulf Stream.

I travelled through the pages. Tobacco and alcoholic drinks. 'Icelanders generally say "Good Health" (*Skal*) each time they raise their glasses when drinking alcohol, at the same time looking into one another's eyes.'

I looked into the eyes of the stewardess and said, '*Skal*.'

She smiled back and I detected warmth behind this smile. But it was a different stewardess.

'Do you know what it means?' she asked.

I shook my head, still warming myself with her smile.

'It means skull. It's different from the Scandinavian. In the old days the Vikings used to cut a skull in half and drink from it.' Her tone implied: Those were the days.

'You seem to approve of drinking more than your colleague.'

'She has had many bad times because of drink.'

'And you have had many good times?'

'Always I have the good times. With or without the drinking.' She, too, spoke with a slight American accent; but her v's became w's and vice versa and some of her s's became sh's. She sat on the arm of the empty gangway seat next to me: there were few passengers on board and she had time to waste. She pointed at my papers. 'You know much about volcanoes?'

'Quite a bit.' I listened to my voice to hear if I could detect its lying quality: I could and hoped she couldn't.

'They are a hobby of yours, these volcanoes?'

I swallowed the vodka neatly and quickly as the Russians had taught me in Moscow. Fire and ice. Perhaps it would oil the lying squeak in my voice. 'It's a little more than a hobby. It's part of my job.'

She said: 'You have come to observe Hekla?'

'That's the general idea.' I held up the empty glass. 'Could I have another, please?'

'Of course. It is wery good wodka, is it not?'

I nodded. 'Wery, wery good. Vonderful, in fact.'

I put away the papers because I didn't want to tax my knowledge of eruptions. The girl returned and sat down again: she seemed to be a rather unorthodox stewardess by BOAC or Pan-Am standards. And the absence of the papers deflected her not one degree. 'You are very lucky that Hekla has erupted again after twenty-three years;' she said.

Press on with the lies, then. Make this a dress rehearsal. But first another dose of fire water – the volcano in the glass. 'I'm going to Iceland at the request of your Government. The ash has poisoned cattle and pastureland. I'm something of an expert on these matters.'

'You must be a very clever man.' The light blue eyes appraised me and I glimpsed formidable singleness of purpose. 'In Iceland girls say, "Brains first, then looks".'

The compliment seem dubious. It was also unanswerable. I examined the cube of ice in my vodka; it had a tiny white Christmas tree imprisoned inside.

She went on: 'If you are lucky you may see Hekla from the aircraft just before we land. You know that in the Middle Ages people thought it was the Gates of Hell?'

At least I knew my Hekla after two days of application in London's museums and libraries. I took out a notebook and read aloud: 'The wailing and gnashing of teeth of the damned can be heard from the mountains and shepherds have seen great vultures driving the fallen souls in the form of black ravens into the opening to hell.'

'Vonderful,' she said.

It didn't seem exactly wonderful. I finished the vodka, Christmas tree and all.

'You would like another?'

'I might as well. Vodka seems to go with volcanoes.'

'It is good that you like vodka. We like it very much in Iceland.'

'So I gather. I don't remember people drinking a lot last time I was there.'

'You have been to Iceland before?'

'During the war.' I didn't mention my recent visit to the NATO base.

She paused – to calculate my age, I suspected. She confirmed the suspicion. 'How old were you then?' It seemed doubtful if Icelandic conversation was ever hampered by reticence.

'I was only a child. My father was in the British Embassy. But I learned to speak Icelandic.'

She exclaimed enthusiastically in Icelandic, which is Old Norse. 'Say something,' she said.

'*Djoffullin sjalfur*,' I said. Which means roughly: 'Bloody Hell'. I added: 'But I prefer to speak English.'

'Vonderful,' she said, and went to fetch some more vodka.

The aircraft was lowering itself on to the grey pastures of cloud as if it wanted to touch down on them. It was the time to stop aeronautical speculation; the time to banish all speculation about the altimeter which would bring us down on the razored peaks of the mountains just below the clouds if . . .

The other passengers were queuing for the toilets. Prematurely fastening their seat belts, extinguishing cigarettes or yawning and scratching with exaggerated nonchalance.

I accepted my third vodka with a buoyant disregard for landing formalities inspired by the two previous vodkas. And – with a familiarity that owed something to the same source – asked the stewardess what her name was.

It was, she said, Gudrun.

We were told to strap ourselves in and stop smoking. We

submerged in the cloud, then surfaced underneath. And there was Iceland – all lichen, moss and black ash from the air. Uncompromising, fighting with the sea in a front-line of breakers. Mountains veined with snow on one side of us, on the other a shower of rain bowling along like a bundle of gnats.

Gudrun sat down and peered towards the mountains. 'It is wery disappointing,' she said. 'I cannot see Hekla.'

She pointed downwards. 'Perhaps you can see Surtsey down there? Iceland, you see, is still forming. It is wery vonderful.'

I looked for the island that had suddenly sprung from the sea in a fountain of fire and smoke. But I couldn't see it.

We sank lower and went into circuit. I mentally recited some of my homework: 'The centre of Iceland consists of a rift from SW to NE. This is part of a vast rift running the length of the Mid-Atlantic Ridge south from Iceland to the Azores, Ascension Island and Tristan da Cunha . . . thought to represent a line of fracture along which the Atlantic Ocean may first have opened . . . from which basalts have been pouring out for millions of years.'

The runway was a few feet below, wet and fast. 'Of the volcanic rocks the tertiary plateau basalts are the oldest dating from Eocene to Pliocene . . .'

We bumped once, then settled and the first sign I saw said: 'US Navy Ops Field Elevation 169 ft'.

I considered asking Gudrun, now in scarlet jacket and hat, out to dinner. But reluctance to invoke a clause of the tired businessman's travel manual prevented me; just such reluctance could make a man an octogenarian celibate.

I said goodbye to her breezily and squeezed past her on to the landing steps. She looked hurt, I thought; but it was too late now. I was on the tarmac and the runway accelerating across the airfield like buckshot.

At the duty-free counters I debated prices with a morose sales assistant so that I could be last through formalities and customs and proceed unnoticed to my own nearby destination.

I was still deep in low finance when Gudrun rounded the corner, a galleon in full sail. She dropped anchor in front of me and said: 'You did not pay for your vodkas.'

Interest animated the face of the sales assistant.

'I'm sorry,' I said, searching my pockets for the kronur I bought at London Airport.

She considered the coins in my hand. 'Why are you staying around like this? Reykjavik is thirty-five kilometres from here and you will miss the bus.'

'I prefer to go by cab.'

'That will cost you much money. You are very rich?'

'Not rich at all.'

'Where are you staying?'

'In a guest-house in Baragata.'

'Then you are certainly not so rich.'

'A lot of scientists stay there. It's very peaceful, I'm told.' I held out the coins. 'Take whatever I owe you.'

'I do not want your money,' she said.

Which was perplexing. My body, perhaps? I put the coins back in my pocket and waited optimistically.

She said: 'Tomorrow I will introduce you to a man who knows all about volcanoes.'

Which was what I needed like a crater in the head.

'Do you know the Saga Hotel?'

I shook my head. 'It wasn't here in my day.'

'You will find it very easily.' Her face challenged me not to find it. 'I shall be there at eight o'clock tomorrow evening. Perhaps the three of us may dine and dance.'

'The three-step?'

'You are not anxious to meet my friend?'

'Not if he's your boyfriend. Perhaps' – consulted the tired

businessman's manual – 'perhaps you and I could have dinner tomorrow at the Saga and meet your friend some other time.'

She smiled as the conversation degenerated into a cliché of her profession. 'Very well.' She paused. 'But what about all those poor cattle dying?'

I looked concerned. Which I supposed I was because I like cattle. And birds, and human beings sometimes. 'There's nothing I can do for them. I can only try and stop it happening again.'

She looked relieved. 'Very well. Eight o'clock in the downstairs bar. We have many things to discuss. And now – can I give you a lift into Reykjavik? I have a little car.'

A single lie spawns with great fertility. I pointed at an Orion P3 anti-submarine surveillance aircraft brushing up wings of spray on the runway. 'I have to meet someone off that plane.'

'Who is he?'

'An American scientist. He's been rushed in. We'll be working together on this project.'

She looked at the unorthodox passenger aircraft with surprise. But the surprise was prevented from being inflated into suspicion by sudden emotion. 'Britain *and* America helping little Iceland,' she said. 'It is vonderful.'

'Wonderful,' I said.

And so it was.

2

Charlie Martz

The NATO base at Keflavik, which also serves as one of the capital's two airfields, once belonged to the British. They occupied it when they occupied Iceland on May 10, 1940, to prevent the Germans doing the same thing. Later in the war the Americans took over the job because Britain had other commitments.

But after the war the Americans were reluctant to leave Iceland vacant for new post-war enemies to occupy and in 1951 Keflavik became a NATO base staffed predominantly by Americans. There are some 2,000 Naval personnel, 1,000 Air Force and *two* Army men.

The welfare authorities do their best. Cinema, theatre, sport, domestic television and radio. But it is difficult to make a site on a lava field homely. In the winter it gets light at 10 a.m. and dark at 2 p.m.; there is a daily announcement of the Chill Factor (temperature multiplied by wind velocity) by which the mathematically-minded can calculate how quickly they could die from exposure; even tourist literature, which can normally transplant a palm tree almost anywhere, admits that Keflavik 'is rather bleak and barren'.

In high summer it never gets dark, which is not such a relief from winter gloom because you can get bored with looking at military buildings, unaffected by the influence of Le Corbusier, and hangars and lava. There is also a possibility of volcanic activity under the base. Many servicemen consider Keflavik to be the worst foreign posting after Vietnam.

Strenuous efforts are also made by the Military to foster goodwill between Americans and Icelanders. These efforts succeed to an extent but there is still some opposition to the 'Army of Occupation' which declined to depart after the war. The United States then argued that the war was not over until an actual peace treaty had been concluded with Germany; In 1946 a new agreement was drawn up permitting the Americans to stay at Keflavik. Opposition to this was fierce and partly responsible for a change in Government. Five years later the tenancy was extended under the auspices of NATO.

The hostility emanates mostly from Communists within the divided People's Union which holds nine of the sixty seats in Parliament. It manifests itself in demonstrations which were recently concentrated against the Americans' own television. They were asked to adjust the transmitter so that Icelanders' artistic appreciation was not debased. Thus the islanders were deprived in one political move of Rawhide, Captain Kangaroo, The Flying Nun and Sergeant Preston of the Yukon. Demonstrators further emphasised their views on American entertainment by entering the base and pouring paint over the TV equipment.

I walked from the civilian air terminal to the entrance to the base. Past raw blocks housing Service families – each apartment a microcosm of Los Angeles or New York City or Seattle, with Chevrolet, Ford or Volkswagen parked outside on concrete or black volcanic ash.

The reception room was a small hothouse occupied by an American military policeman, scrubbed and stroppy and gingery, and an Icelandic policeman in black uniform playing patience. An invisible barrier preventing communication stood between them and on the wall hung a Pam-Am calendar displaying a coloured photograph of Novodevichy Monastery in Moscow.

I spoke to the American guard, as resentful as a dog with bitten ears. 'I think I'm expected . . .'

He interrupted me with a jerk of his thumb towards the young Icelandic policeman, picked up the phone and embarked on a wearily obscene conversation with someone called Irwin.

'My name's Conran,' I said. 'I believe Commander Martz is expecting me.'

The military policeman stopped talking on the phone and accused me headily through his spectacles. Why hadn't I told him who it was I wanted? He said: 'I'll call you back, Irwin.' But by that time the Icelandic policeman had spoken to Charlie Martz and put an eight of hearts under a nine of clubs.

We drove to Martz's Nissen hut offices in a Land Rover. British hut, British truck.

He called for coffee, offered cigarettes, put one foot on his desk, flashed a gold tooth somewhere at the back of his mouth, called me 'an old son of a gun' a couple of times, massaged the chopped stalks of his harvested hair and inquired with totally spurious concern about the flight, the weather in London and my health.

On his desk were several files, a photograph of his wife and kids and, unaccountably, a toilet roll. On the walls of the office, built austerely for war, were pictures of Charlie Martz with John Kennedy, Charlie Martz with various admirals, Charlie Martz with the boys. Charlie Martz ostensibly in the carefree days before they shore-based him and lumbered him with security and liaison – and British agents.

But he was a nice man, was Charlie. Fortyish, intensively off-duty in windcheater and concertina slacks, with a broad, frank face that was his greatest asset – I was never quite sure how devious he was behind his props. Or at what stage in the pictorial history of Charlie Martz boyishly displayed on the walls his training in counter-espionage, and perhaps espionage, had begun. Anyway he still looked as if there should have been a compass or a periscope instead of a desk in front of him.

Currently Charlie was trying to equate liaison with counterespionage. As liaison officer he spent much time trying to convince a phlegmatic world that great camaraderie was burgeoning between American and Icelander: as a counter-espionage expert he had called in a British agent to help him stamp out subversion. The equation didn't equate and now he gave up.

'Bill, old buddy,' he said, 'it's gotten worse.'

'How much worse?'

'Lots worse.'

'You mean they've painted your TV cameras again?'

'Nothing like that.'

The painting had occurred just after my last visit. I had been flown in by the United States Air Force for a briefing and returned to London to await developments without even seeing Reykjavik.

Martz walked to the window and stared in the direction of the herring-filled sea. Momentarily back at the helm. He said: 'We calculate that there are now thirty-five Russians in Reykjavik. Thirty-five, Bill, for a population of 200,000.'

'You mean diplomats?'

'Diplomats and their families and staff.' He lit a cigarette with a gun-metal, wind-shielded lighter. 'And as if that were not enough, Goddamnit, the news agency *Novisti* is starting operations here. At the moment the Soviets are occupying seven buildings in Reykjavik, not to mention some rooms let to them by the Poles.'

'At least you know where they all are.' So far the only difference to the situation on my previous visit three months earlier was numerical.

Martz sat down again and replaced his foot on the desk. 'That's just the Goddamn trouble, Billy boy, we don't.'

'But diplomats can't take off and strike camp on Vatna Jökull.'

'Diplomats can't. Spies can.' He paused. 'You remember all the stories about the Germans landing agents here during the last war to start a Fifth Column?'

'They weren't just stories. The British found transmitters in caves in the north-east on the Langanes Peninsula. They also landed some Icelanders who had been living in Berlin. They thought they'd got them brainwashed, but they hadn't – the *agents* went straight to the local police. We reckon the Soviets are trying something similar right now.'

'To little old Iceland?'

'Little old Iceland nothin'. The key to the North Atlantic more like. And as you know, Bill' – he dropped the old buddy when things were getting really serious – 'the Soviets think a long way ahead. They're seeing another war five, ten, twenty years ahead. Or maybe next year. And they want to have a great big foot in Iceland if and when that war comes.'

'What evidence have you that the Russians are landing agents?'

'Nothing hard until the other day. A lot of indications though. As you know there's been a lot of Soviet Naval activity around these shores. Not to mention the fishing fleets. They call it Red Square now up on the East Coast.'

Still nothing that we hadn't covered on my previous visit. 'So?'

'Every now and again a Soviet trawler puts into a fiord

claiming a breakdown or something. By the time our guys or the Icelanders get there the engine has been put right and more than likely a passenger is missing somewhere in Iceland. And there's another funny thing . . .' He waited to give the funny thing more effect.

'What funny thing is that?'

'According to the guys who reach the Soviet trawlers none of the crews ever smelt of fish.'

Silently we ruminated on the olfactory evidence. Rain machine-gunned the corrugated-iron roof. A 727 came in low from the sea looking for the glistening canal that was the runway.

Finally I said: 'Perhaps they use deodorant.'

Charlie Martz said: 'Perhaps.' The way you humour a facetious child. Then he said: 'There's one anchored some-where near Vopnafjorthur right now if you'd like to go and have a looksee.'

'Okay. But surely you've got a little more to go on than Russian fishermen who don't smell of fish.'

We eyed each other across the toilet roll. Allies playing poker. A common cause but different methods, different personalities, miserly with our secrets, lavish with suspicion.

'There is a bit more,' he said reluctantly.

'This is killing you, isn't it?'

The bonhomie had departed for a while, an unwanted guest. He eyed me with resignation because I wasn't his sort of agent; maybe he didn't even like me; maybe my dossier – perhaps it was in one of the files on the table – didn't appeal to him. Something like: 'First assignment since crack-up, fondness for drink and women increased since this breakdown, flippant in manner, invaluable to this project because of his knowledge of Iceland and Icelandic. Hobbies – ornithology.' For Christ's sake – a bird watcher!

I said: 'Look, Charlie, if we're going to do this job we've

got to do it together. If you don't want me to share your secrets why in God's name did you send for me?'

'You know why I asked for you. Not you in particular. But a limey.'

'Because there are a lot of Icelanders around who wouldn't take too kindly to an American nosing among their affairs?'

'Something like that.'

'Well, you got me and you'd better come clean or I might as well catch the next plane home.'

'Okay,' he said, reaching for straws of friendliness. 'Five days ago a Russian agent was picked up at Egilsstathir. How's that for openers?'

'Not bad,' I said. 'Not bad at all.'

'At least we *think* he was a Russian agent.'

'Ah.'

'But we can't be sure.'

'Why can't you be sure?'

'Because he's dead,' Martz said.

The difficult part was over now and Martz began to talk with something like his usual loquacity.

'As you probably know,' Martz said, 'Egilsstathir is one of the few places in Iceland with any trees. Or the forest at Hallormsstathur rather. A local cop was out rambling or something when he came across signs of human habitation. The ashes of a fire, a gnawed bone, that sort of thing.'

'Wasn't there snow up there?'

'Not in the Lagarfljot valley. Anyway the lawman got angry because it seems he reckons that part of the forest belongs to him. So he waited around. After about an hour this guy comes up carrying a sleeping bag and a radio transmitter. The cop came out of hiding and challenged him but he ran for it. The cop called on him to stop but he just kept on running. Then a shooting match started.'

'You see, we nature-lovers can be quite tough when we feel like it.'

'Yeah.' He explored the stubble on his scalp with the tips of his fingers. 'Yeah, I guess so. Anyway this cop must have been quite a marksman because he holed our spy right between the eyes with a pistol from seventy-five yards.'

'That wasn't very clever,' I said.

'I didn't say it was very clever.' Martz did a reconnaissance patrol of his study and sat down again.

'Any identification papers?'

Martz nodded. 'All Icelandic. Ingolfur Gislason. Forgeries – but good ones. Someone by that name was expected to rent a room in Egilsstathir the day after he was killed. The landlord still had the letter signed Gislason.'

'Where was it posted?'

'In Reykjavik.'

'And the transmitter and sleeping bag?'

'Swedish and Danish respectively. But that doesn't mean a damn thing. You can buy both in Iceland.'

'Then why the hell do you think he was Russian?'

'There had been a Soviet trawler anchored off the coast the day before. About forty miles away. The crew of a C-130 reckoned they saw a man heading across the snow from the trawler in the direction of Egilsstathir.'

'I thought you said there wasn't any snow up there?'

'There's plenty of it outside the valley. The roads are still impassable up north.'

'And that's the only evidence you have that the dead man was a Russian?'

'As I told you we've suspected for some time that they've been landing agents like the Germans did. This is the nearest we've got to proof. I reckon Mr Gislason spoke fluent Icelandic, had a prepared Icelandic background and contacts to back up his stories just like a British agent parachuted in to France in 1941 would have contacts in the Resistance.'

'Do you have any ideas?'

'Our Mr Sigurdson does.'

'Who the devil is he?'

'My opposite number in the Icelandic police. Liaison with the Americans and counter-subversion. The trouble is he gets a little confused as to who the enemy is. He wants the Russians out but he's not crazy about having the Americans in.'

'What are Mr Sigurdson's ideas?'

'He had two suspects. He was keeping them under surveillance. Waiting for an agent to contact them. He had nothing definite on them – just Icelandic intuition.' Martz's voice implied that this was a formidable quality. 'They're both Communists, both highly mobile. They've both had dealings with the Russians and the Czechs.'

'What do you mean *had* two suspects?' Martz issued his information in cliff-hangers.

'He's now got three.'

'Ah.'

'Sigurdson flew up to Egilsstathir immediately after the shooting. On a slip of paper among Gislason's forged documents he found a name – Hafstein.'

Which was a relief in a country where the second names are so alike that phone numbers are listed under Christian names. 'And who is Hafstein?'

'It seems he's a guy working in the national register – the Thjodskrain. It figures. That way the Soviets could plant forged birth certificates and other documents confirming their agents' identities if they ever came under suspicion.'

In the adjoining office someone battered on Martz's door and a voice bawled: 'You in there, Charlie?'

The other Charlie Martz bawled back: 'Sure am, Harry. What can I do for you?'

The door opened and a basketball player's head about 6 ft

4 ins from the ground looked around. Appraised me, dismissed me and concentrated on Martz. 'You working late or something?'

'Something like that, Harry. This is Bill Conran, an old buddy of mine from London, England.'

Harry smiled at me because I was Martz's buddy and swivelled back towards Martz. 'Well, when you've finished get your fat ass out of that chair and buy me a beer. Bring Mr Conran along too.'

'Not tonight, Harry, you old sonofabitch. You buy me one tomorrow, eh?'

Harry grimaced, shrugged, shut the door; we heard his retreating voice decrying Martz's unsocial behaviour in fundamental terms.

Martz stretched in his swivel chair. 'Great guy, Harry. We were on a destroyer together once.' He finished stretching and became the wary raconteur again. 'Anything else you want to know?'

'I suppose I'd better make contact with Mr Sigurdson.'

'He's expecting you. He's not the most forthcoming of guys because he reckons Icelandic security should be left to Icelanders. He has a point, I guess – if there were enough Icelanders to do the job. And if they had an Army . . .'

'What's he like apart from that?'

'You'll like him. A great drinker, a great joker – like most Icelanders. But cunning beneath it all.'

'Not unlike Charlie Martz.'

'That's not kind,' Martz said. The sun came out and discovered his gold tooth.

'Was there nothing else at all to confirm that Gislason was a Russian?'

'As a matter of fact there was. He had a steel tooth. You should know those teeth' – Martz was telling me that he knew I'd worked in Moscow – 'like a mouthful of bullets.'

I did know those teeth because it had once cost me £100

to go to Helsinki to avoid Russian dentistry. 'How the hell did the Russians overlook that?'

Martz shrugged. 'God knows. But there it was, at the back of his lower jaw.'

But it didn't really surprise me. The KGB was both the most efficient and inefficient network in the world. Machiavellian intrigue hampered by strokes of wondrous incompetence.

Martz stood up and replaced the mask that faced the world. 'Come on, Billy boy, let's go take a look at that spy ship.'

In Iceland the weather can change by the minute. Now the sky was ice-blue and clear of cloud. We walked across the tarmac to the waiting C-130.

Beneath me Iceland. Twice in one day. It was 10 p.m. and the heavens were as blue-bright as if it were 10 a.m. Behind us the playing cards of Reykjavik, below the black and khaki moss, ahead the mountains finding the snow as they grew taller.

Then I saw Hekla – and heard her above the drilling of the Hercules' engines. An umbrella of smoke and a turbulence of clouds: and beneath all this the red mouths spewing lava into the sky. It was difficult to see the craters in detail because of the smoke, but from the aircraft the earth's crust looked very frail.

Martz had similar feelings. 'Makes you feel pretty puny, doesn't it?' he shouted.

'It makes what we're doing seem even more puny,' I shouted back. 'Can't we get any nearer? Get under that smoke?'

'Are you crazy?'

We left Hekla behind and took up the northern boundaries of Vatna Jökull, the largest glacier in Europe. In 1783 the Laki fissure had erupted west of this glacier poisoning sheep, horses and cattle and killing twenty per cent of Iceland's population through famine. The peaks and caverns of the Ice Age, discarded by time, accepted a bluish glow from the sky. Then we were over its last white fingers, groping as ponderously as evolution itself.

The Hercules dipped towards the coast and we sat back in the old leather seats. The aircraft banked and we looked down at a fiord, the water motionless inside its mountain barricades. In the middle, just getting up steam, was the Russian trawler looking as innocent as a pleasure boat on Lake Lucerne, a red flag flying pertly from her mast.

Martz made an extravagant gesture towards her; the gesture could have been triumphant in the face of my scepticism, or defeatist because they were getting away.

We went as low as the mountains would allow and the little men on the deck waved at us.

'Will she get intercepted?' I yelled at Martz.

'She might' His voice implied that the interception would be pretty futile.

We did another circuit, then headed back across the primeval countryside. It was 11.25 p.m. and as we settled down over the capital the sun was just going down, ready to bounce up again without letting dusk make night. The sea was bronze, wheeling with seagulls. And Reykjavik, which means Smoky Bay – so named because of the steam from the hot springs noticed by the Norse settlers in 874 – looked very innocent from the air with its churches and clean houses and small waves losing themselves on its shores.

'So now I'd better find Sigurdson,' I shouted at Martz on the tarmac, forgetting that there was no longer any need to raise my voice.

'Don 't worry about that Billy boy – he'll find you.'

The prospect pleased him because he clapped me on the back with one large hand.

'Does he know all about me? My cover and everything?'

'He sure does. And I hope you know your subject because Icelanders are very inquisitive. Very friendly, very inquisitive, very tough. They also like to tell you about their dreams. But then you know all that.'

'I was only a kid,' I said.

'You'll have to go up and take a look at Hekla, seeing as that's supposed to be the reason you're here.'

'Yes,' I said. 'And do some bird watching at the same time.' Just to re-activate his doubts.

We stopped outside his Nissen hut. It wasn't the most august building on the base. Perhaps he had been relegated to it when the mob of students subverted the barbed-wire fences and painted the TV cameras.

The weather did a quick-change and the rain returned.

'Okay,' he said. 'Now the car and the gun and the little bugging devices they seem to think you're so clever with.'

The car was a pale green Chevrolet, the gun a Smith & Wesson.

'Anything more?' he asked.

'I wouldn't say no to some ammunition.'

The old-buddy smile once again erased the doubts. 'Jesus, I nearly forgot.' He gave me a box of bullets. 'Nothing intentional.' He shook my hand. 'Good luck, Billy boy. See you tomorrow. Be good.'

I released my hand and smiled because I liked Charlie Martz. 'And you,' I said.

I started the Chevrolet and headed across the lava field in the direction of Smoky Bay.

3

The Welcome

The initial greetings to a country affect your whole stay. They lodge in your brain and stay there until you leave. At least there was no doubt about the spirit of the greeting on the way to Reykjavik from Keflavik. And it nearly did lodge in my brain – permanently.

It happened somewhere near the hill called Stapi which is reputed to be haunted – Icelanders are much affected by wights and ghosts and the toughest put away their muscles when the Huldufolk are mentioned.

There was nothing ghostly about the bullet. The sea was on my left, the lava field stretching away to my right, more desolate than any desert. The rain bounced on the bonnet, the wipers moved like metronomes. Then, crack, the metronomes were wiping glass cracked into a million sugar cubes and there was a hole the size of a new potato just above my head.

I braked, skidded slightly, stopped and crouched on the floor. The bullet, which had ricocheted around inside the car, lay on the passenger seat, warm and bright and hardly scratched. I crawled to the passenger side, opened the door and lay on the ground.

Then I reached up, took the Smith & Wesson from the glove compartment and peered round the fender. There was a lava mound ahead, greeny-brown and cracking at the top, scaled with lichen and cushioned with moss round the base. I guessed that the sniper was behind it; but there wasn't much I could do about it unless he showed himself; if I showed myself in the all-night light or tried to drive away then I was dead.

I glanced at my watch. Midnight, June 30th.

I took aim from behind the wheel and potted one of the cubes of pumice on top of the mound. Fairground stuff. I thought I detected a movement behind the mound but I couldn't be sure. The rain bowled down the long empty road plastered my clothes to my body. It was going to be a question of whose patience became exhausted first.

Then a pair of headlights showed in the uncertain light about a mile down the road. There was a movement behind the lava mound and I potted another chunk of lava; the marksman must have seen the headlights and realised that the driver would stop. He was probably backing away into the bleak cover behind.

The headlights stopped, rain lancing their beams. It was a red Broncho truck. I stood up and prayed; nothing happened. I explained to the driver – an old seaman by the look of him – that a pebble had struck the windscreen. And before he noticed the bullet-hole I punched out the frosted glass.

Then I drove on to Reykjavik past lines of dried fish hanging out like laundry, past the new Swiss aluminium plant at Straumsvik. With the windscreen gone it was like driving underwater. The houses and apartment blocks of the capital looked very welcome and I congratulated Ingolfur Arnarson, the first settler, on his choice.

The house in Baragata, near the city centre, was white

and old, surrounded by an uncertain lawn of new grass. The landlady was still up; so, it seemed, was half of Reykjavik. She welcomed me and in a series of shambling little sentences assured me that the weather had been fine until my arrival, described the eruption of Hekla and deplored the consumption of strong drink.

She showed me my ground-floor room, whisked me upstairs for the inevitable coffee, treated me to flurry of comment on young people's morals – it was their parents' fault – and then allowed me to return to my room because I must be tired.

When I opened the door there was a crate of ginger ale and soda water on the floor and two bottles on the table dividing the single beds. And a man sitting in the wicker-work chair.

He grinned and began to stand up.

'Don't get up,' I said. 'You're Mr Sigurdson, I believe.'

The grin faltered a little.

Einar Sigurdson looked as tough as a trawlerman. About forty with a broad face, smiling creases from nose to mouth, a round scar on his neck, faded eyes and longish pale hair cut at an awkward length around the sides so that it stuck out. But Sigurdson was not a man who needed to bother with the fripperies of fashion: his strengths were deep in his searching eyes, rasping in his voice, sheathed in his ordinary suit. He was a man's man and a lady's man.

He was also an exuberant man. He proceeded with the grin, grasping my fingers with one hand, my bicep with the other. 'It is good to see you,' he said; his bluff sincerity was more convincing than Charlie Martz's. 'Welcome to Iceland.'

'I've already been welcomed.' I showed him the bullet, snug in my hand.

'You were shot at?' Incredulity, mirth and concern contended for dominance.

'I was.'

He disposed of the incredulity, briefly proffered the concern, then indulged the mirth. 'You seem to be very accident prone,' he said.

How much did he know of Moscow? I wondered. 'I don't call a bullet through the windscreen an accident.'

'But you are alive and that is vonderful.'

'Wery,' I said.

'We must drink to that.'

'Isn't it a little late?'

'It is never too late to do anything in Iceland. To drink or make the love. At least not in the summer when we have no night. In the winter it is different – then we sleep. I have here a bottle of aquavit and a bottle of Black Death.'

'That sounds interesting.'

'It's like schnapps. Once upon the time it was forbidden to stick a gay label on a bottle of liquor so they stuck this black one on – that is how it got its name. You like to try?'

'All right,' I said. I didn't recall Black Death in my child-hood.

He poured half an inch of colourless liquid in a thick glass for me and an inch of aquavit for himself. He topped up the aquavit with ginger ale. 'We call that asni – it means mule. We Icelanders like a long drink. You would like some ginger ale?'

'No,' I said. 'I'll take it neat.' Like I had once taken a Stolichnaya, oily from a deep freeze, and woken up much later far from home. You didn't necessarily learn from your mistakes: but then I didn't really care any more.

'Skal,' he said.

'Skal,' I said. It was like vodka, only faintly aromatic.

He swallowed half his mule and examined the little whitewashed room. 'I have been here some time,' he said. 'The front door is open always. When you came down just now I took myself to the toilet.'

'Couldn't you have asked the landlady if you could wait?'

He shook his head violently so that the pale hair swung across his forehead. 'She is the enemy. A member of the International Order of Good Templars. They are teetotallers and they are very influential in this country of ours. It is,' he added unnecessarily, 'a country of extremes. Your lady would have smelled the drink on my breath and banished me from her house.' He finished his drink and poured us both another. 'We must be very quiet.' He raised his glass and stared into my eyes guide-book style.

I sipped at death and said: 'Okay, Einar, let's be quiet and get down to business. I've got a lot of questions I want to ask you.'

'And I have a lot to ask you. First of all, why do you wish to help the Bandarizkur?' He put a pillow against the wall and lay down on one of the beds, asni beside him, hands behind his sturdy neck.

'You speak as if I were helping a Nazi in the last war. Are they so unpopular, the Americans?'

He shook his head, fringing his forehead again. 'No. We like them. They are wonderful people. But not all Icelanders want them here. It is, after all, our country. Although it is a little country and we realise that we cannot make the rules.'

'They are here to protect you.'

'Would they be here to protect us if we were not in such a – how do you say it? – strategic position?'

I applied myself to my Black Death without answering.

He went on: 'And would Britain have been so keen to protect us in 1940 if we hadn't been in such a position of strategy?'

'It doesn't alter the fact that you're a member of NATO and the military presence of the Americans is desirable to shield a fellow member.' I poured myself another drink to dispel the diplomatic clichés – if there was one thing I disliked more than diplomats it was their clichés. 'Would you rather have the Russians here?'

'We would rather just have Icelanders here.'

'If you don't have the Americans then as sure as night is day in Iceland you'll have the Soviets.'

'You are right, of course.' He considered the gloomy truth. 'That is why I have agreed to help you.'

He passed me a copy of the morning newspaper, *Morgunbladid*, with four sentences underlined—

Despite progress in military technology the Atlantic Ocean is still very important militarily. Icelanders must keep this in mind when they think about their own security. They must also keep an open eye on those that now seek a position on the Atlantic, i.e. the Soviet Union. Isn't its increased interest in Iceland a clear witness to that?

Sigurdson mixed himself another asni and said: 'You see, my friend, we realise the truth. But that doesn't stop us wishing that we were not a prawn in the Big Power Game.'

'Pawn,' I said. 'But in any case that's a pro-Government newspaper.'

'I am trying to give you a complete picture,' he said, and handed me a copy of the Opposition paper *Timinn*. It described a protest march which halted predictably outside the American Embassy. There a student 'challenged all imperialists and preached world revolution'.

He also handed me the Communist paper *Thjodviljinn* which described the protest march and added for good measure: 'It is now the task of the young to join the occupation opponents and relieve the nation of the yoke of the occupation.'

'You see?' Sigurdson said.

'I see.'

'We are very democratic.'

I read a bit more of *Morgunbladid* because it contained a report on the Hekla fall-out. 'Tests of samples taken of ash from the Hekla eruption indicate that the fluor contents are much higher than in the eruption of 1947. Sheep on a number of farms in the vicinity of Hekla have become sick, and it is suspected that they suffer from acute fluor poisoning.'

Perhaps I would be helping Iceland more by applying myself to my spurious rather than my true profession.

The bed creaked as Sigurdson, curious to see what had caught my interest, came up behind me. I could feel his gun inside his heavy grey jacket pressed against my back.

'Ah yes, Hekla,' he said. 'We have the finest volcanoes in the world. Always they are erupting. Now you are going to pretend to investigate Hekla's poison, yesh?'

The s slushed into sh and the slight American accent reminded me of Gudrun.

'I might even do some good,' I said.

'Rid poor little Iceland of two poisons, eh? The Russians and the fluor.'

I wondered how unpleasant he became in drink. He sat down abruptly and laughed with great vigour until tears of aquavit rolled down his pale cheeks.

I remembered reading something about the Icelandic love of laughter. 'Simple humour and witty ditties' – or something like that. Sigurdson seemed to possess his countryman's characteristics in abundance: he was hospitable, generous, tough, boastful, neurotic about his country's size and its appeal to America and Russia. He was probably also appreciative of witty ditties: I didn't know yet whether he was a good policeman.

He stopped laughing, wiped his cheeks with a white silk handkerchief and said: 'The Communists are not so strong here – it is just that they make a lot of noise.'

'Strong and noisy enough to persuade a mob to wreck

the American TV equipment at the base. Perhaps strong enough to persuade a mob to do far worse.'

'One or two are strong,' he admitted. 'But not the ones the public read about.'

'Do you know who they are?'

He looked at me with a shrewdness that was startling because laughter-lines still cobwebbed the corners of his eyes. I imagined him laughing hugely as he shot a fugitive in the back. 'You know I know,' he said.

'All right, I know you know.'

'One in particular,' he said. 'A man named Hafstein.' He opened a black briefcase and tossed three folders on the table. 'There are the dossiers on all three of them.'

I decided that he was probably a very good policeman.

After that the seriousness evaporated. As if we had concluded the first day of business conference and the night was young.

He poured me an inch of Black Death and an inch and a half of asni for himself. 'We will finish these,' he said, pointing at the two bottles, now half empty – or half full, according to your approach to life. 'Then perhaps we will go and find some girls. There are many beautiful girls in Reykjavik and there are not so many men. We will go perhaps to the Loftleidir or the Saga.'

'Not tonight,' I said. 'Thanks all the shame.' The Black Death was melting my pronunciation into awful jokes.

Sigurdson laughed massively, although no flesh shook on his hard body. And I – Noel Coward and Brendan Behan fused into one – laughed with him.

'Thanks all the shame,' he said, and threw himself back on the bed. Somewhere beneath him there was a crack of protesting woodwork. He sat upright again, put his fingers to his lips. 'Shush.'

We winked at each other and I mixed myself an asni with Black Death. I liked Charlie Martz, I liked Einar

Sigurdson, I loved Gudrun. 'Here's to Anglo-Icelandic friendship.'

We drank to that. Then to American-Icelandic friendship. Then to Anglo-American friendship. Then we ran out of liquor.

We squeezed the bottles but not a drop issued forth. We commiserated with each other and would have sung if it hadn't been for the International Templar upstairs.

Finally Sigurdson rose to his feet, put one arm round my shoulders, hugged me and announced: 'I like you.'

I nodded and we both knew that the nod embraced all that was decent in the relationships of mankind. 'And I like you, old buddy,' I said.

'*Bles*,' he said.

I watched him walk down the road in a series of S bends. Then I undressed, picked up the three dossiers and went to bed. When I awoke at 10 a.m. I was still cuddling the dossiers – and a small volcano was erupting inside my skull.

4

The Saga

The description fitted my physical and mental condition. 'A picture of erratic ruin where the entire district looks as if it had been baked, broiled, burnt and boiled by some devilish hand until its chemical soul had fled and left nought behind save a grim, grey shroud of darkness and despair.' It was an old description of a lava field.

I put down the book, rejected my landlady's offer of bread and apricot jam, swallowed my fifth black coffee and went out into the drizzling morning. I took the car to a garage to get the windscreen replaced, then wandered dazedly around the city centre.

It hadn't changed much and darts of memory from child-hood opened small wounds of regret for what might have been. Austurvollur Square was still toytown with the little white Lutheran Cathedral and the Althing – the diminutive Parliament building. In the streets around the square the same bookshops, glossy with Icelandic geography and culture from the time of the sagas to the contemporary Nobel Prize winner Halldor Laxness. Chanting newspaper boys, a policeman in white peaked cap and gloves, teenagers

in flared trousers and brown and fawn sweaters, no hoardings, no dogs, all in miniature.

The tour of the middle-aged schoolboy with a hangover
continued. Along Laufasvegur, overlooking the artificial lake
with its mossy waters and placid ducks, to the American
Embassy, white, two-storeyed, with a Plymouth station
wagon and a black Chrysler New Yorker R18461 parked
outside.

On to the British Ambassador's house. No. 33. A seaside
boarding house with a long garden in front. Then the British
Embassy, white with a turreted roof and a Land Rover with
CD plates outside.

Diplomats. Frightened men acting a charade of manners
that encouraged Russians and Chinese in their barbarism.
A 'strongly-worded note' to deflect an armoured column;
an umbrella to answer a rifle; petulant anachronisms pitted
against inexorable brutality.

A face appeared at the window. Smooth hair with a
self-conscious curl falling over the forehead. White shirt
and striped tie.

We stared at each other briefly, recognition dawning
across the long garden. Jefferey, the one diplomat who
personified my views on his profession. Jefferey, the one
man who knew every detail about my recall from Moscow.

Jefferey in Iceland . . . I turned abruptly and returned
to the lake and looked at the occupants. Duck, geese, swans
and Arctic tern. Before returning to the Serpentine I hoped
to visit Lake Myvatn in the north to have a look at Barrow's
Goldeneye, the harlequin and the scaup.

After Moscow I had relaxed watching birds. These were
the diplomatic birds – coots, whimbrels, pipits, white
wagtails, snipe, shoveler and shag. And the Russians –
red-throated diver, slavonian grebe, red-breasted merganser,
redwing, raven.

The weather changed as if another slide had been slotted

into the projector. Toytown was suddenly warm and stirring in spring sunshine and a breeze crinkled the lake and ruffled the birds' plumage.

The Stolichnaya vodka had tasted all right. A little thick from the deep-freeze but that was all. I had split many such a bottle with a Russian suckled on grain spirit and watched his face turn mauve before mine.

But this one drunk with a Russian playwright in an apartment just off Kutuzovsky Prospect was something special. A Micky Finnovitch.

The room where I regained consciousness was classically bare with a couple of chairs, a leaning dressing-table, a rush mat, a portrait of Lenin – and a bed on which the girl, wearing only a black suspender belt and stockings, and myself were lying. As I swam through the haze I thought: 'At least they haven't planted a man.'

She was very white, heavy-breasted with a Caesarean scar just above the pubic hair. The cameraman said 'Just one more' in Russian; she opened her legs and that was that. She began to dress, looking more attractive as she put on more clothes.

They handed me my clothes. 'Is there anything more?' I asked.

'No, Gaspadeen Conran, you are free to go.'

'When will the prints be ready?'

'Tonight at the latest.' He smiled. 'It is a pity you were asleep for most of the time. But we can retouch the pictures.'

'Can you do an extra set of prints for me?'

'Of course, if you wish. We shall be printing very many sets. *Dosividaniya*, Gaspadeen Conran.'

The first print showed me suspended between two men outside the café, apparently drunk. Then a series which would have fetched good money in parts of Soho or 42nd Street.

'These should be the subject of a private member's bill,' I said.

Jefferey, from the British Embassy, didn't smile. He said: 'There's nothing for it but to ship you out on the next plane.' He examined one of the prints closely.

'Jealous, Jefferey?'

'You always were an offensive sort of man.'

'Only because you didn't like the work I was doing. Trying to unbotch your botch-ups.'

'I imagine these will finish you,' he said. 'You don't exactly look like an absent-minded professor.' A tiny smile humanised his petulantly handsome face.

'You want to try these methods some time,' I said. 'They work, you see. Simple, brutal, amateurish, effective. The Russians could finish the lot of you if they wanted to. But they don't want to – you're too bloody useful to them sending your notes and eating strawberries on the Queen's birthday. Don't you see, Jefferey' – his name should have been Cholmondeley – 'you're out of date? All of you.'

'At least we don't get caught *in flagrante delicto*, old boy.' He had a liking for the French or Latin phrase, did Jefferey.

'Not even the Russians could manage that with you,' I said.

They also sent a set to my wife. She said she understood and started divorce proceedings one year later.

After the 'crack-up' they took me back into the department in Whitehall. Then sent me to Iceland because I was the only one who knew the country and could speak the language; and because no Icelander would see anything compromising in a compromising photograph.

A DC-3 dropped slowly on to the runway of the city airfield and a duck took off from the lake.

I opened my briefcase, took out the dossiers and began to read beside toytown's looking-glass lake.

The memoranda had been typed in Icelandic for my personal information with explanatory comments.

'*Suspect No. 1.* Emil Hafstein. Aged fifty-two, pseudo-intellectual, supports the People's Union, one-time Communist but not ostensibly a fanatical one. There is no stigma in Communism in Iceland. Bachelor with a room in Reykjavik and a house in Hveragerdi forty-six kilometres from Reykjavik. Hobbies – ornithology and the study of Iceland's ancient churches. Suspicions about him hardened since discovery of his name on person of Gislason. In key position to introduce forged documents into Iceland's statistical records. Under observation and has been seen to enter the Russian Chancery building in Gardastraeti on two occasions staying ten minutes and fifteen minutes.' A photograph accompanied the dossier. A thin, guarded face with a goatee beard and sagging neck muscles. The face of a recluse who had not succeeded in finding an escape from life and had, perhaps, sought an ideology as a substitute.

I stared across the lake in the direction of the Russian Embassy. There was really no escape anywhere in the world. Moscow, New York, London, Rwanda and Burundi, toytown . . . the war in which so few were really interested went remorselessly on. Jefferey, the Russians: perhaps it was all being set up again for me.

'*Suspect No. 2.* Valdimar Laxdal. Aged forty-five. Communist but again not apparently fanatical. Political views possibly motived by mercenary considerations. Owns two Cessnas which he hires on charter. A skilled pilot able to fly to inaccessible areas. (This was underlined, with the implica-tion that he could pick up fugitive spies.) Married with two children but marriage believed to be breaking up because of his womanising ways . . .'

Womanising ways, I thought. Come op Einar Sigurdson.

'. . . Recently visited Warsaw and Moscow on a tour arranged by the Communist Party. High standard of living not quite accounted for by his income from chartering small aircraft. Recent deposits, heavier than usual (cash) in the Landsbanki Islands.'

No explanation was given for the suspicion that Laxdal had attracted. But when I looked at his photograph I conceded that no explanation was necessary. The handsome face of a mercenary dedicated to one cause – Valdimar Laxdal. Watch your wife, your wine and your wallet.

'Suspect No. 3. Olav Magnusson. Trawler owner. Aged fifty. Home in Heimaey in the Westman Islands. One of the rich Left Wing supporters. In fact there are no poor Communists in Iceland because there are no really poor people. This invalidates the theory that it is poverty that spawns Communism . . . (I offer no theory for the existence of Communism in a wealthy country except that it is the voice of protest . . .)'

Einar Sigurdson getting in his bit about the 'Army of occupation'.

'. . . Wealthy, running a Mercedes on the mainland and a Saab in Heimaey. Took active part in the Cod War against Britain. Runs mink farm as a sideline. Married with two children in the early twenties. Physically very strong. Suspicions first aroused when US reconnaissance aircraft noted a rendezvous between a Soviet trawler and one of his ships 100 miles east of Gerpir.'

Charlie Martz, I thought, you forgot to tell me that. Magnusson's photograph confirmed his potted biography. Sleek, wealthy, strong.

Sigurdson had appended a note: 'It is imperative that we do not arouse the suspicions of any of these men. If we do, then we shall have lost all chance of breaking the network. Suggest your investigations start with the key man, Hafstein. Good hunting.'

For which I thanked Einar Sigurdson. So far, apart from the dossiers, his only contribution to the investigation had been the presentation of a hangover that made any work impossible.

I strolled back into the centre of town and sent a cable to London. I didn't relish the reply. Then I went back to bed.

5

The Saga of the Saga

The wallpaper was gold, the receptionists attractive and healthy-looking, the general impression of the Saga Hotel as tubular and modern as a memorial to Mr Hilton or Mr Sheraton.

The barmen shook, rattled and stirred with professional detachment. I counted four bars but there could have been more. From upstairs you could see the midnight – or 11.23 p.m. – sun hurry down over the bay. And you could see the geometric patterns of the new Reykjavik.

I banished the memory of Black Death, ordered a Scotch and waited for Gudrun. Around the ground-floor bar long drinks of vodka, gin, brandy and whisky made their impression on expense accounts and ice cubes jingled like money.

Soon the women began to arrive. Of all ages, all sizes. Smart, watchful, on the prowl like the men of other countries. A woman of about fifty, wearing her age and her sequins well, stood next to me and ordered three brandies with ginger ale. She smiled at me and I smiled back. Widow, divorcee, spinster, wife? Here you couldn't tell.

'American?' she asked.

'No, English.'

'Ah, *Brezkur*.' I couldn't tell whether this was good or bad.

She nodded pleasantly, took her drinks and went back to her table to tell her friends the good or bad news. When I turned round they all smiled. Flirtatious, maternal, predatory, or just friendly – I still couldn't tell.

The girls were very smart, a predominance of blondes, wearing mini-skirts and low-cut trouser suits with flared trousers. They came in twos and threes then drifted into larger groups like leaves on a pond.

Most of the men were visitors from abroad eyeing the talent with furtive wonderment or, if they were with colleagues, discussing the profusion of riches with dirty-joke laughter. The local men knew the set-up and left it till later. One moustachioed man in his late twenties sat at a table with eight girls. He seemed unconcerned at his good fortune: he might have been attending a union meeting.

Gudrun's bosom nuzzled me gently in the chest. 'Hallo, Mr Conran,' she said.

'Hallo,' I said.

'I'm sorry I'm early,' she said.

I shrugged.

'It is wonderful to see you. Now please you will buy me a drink.'

I bought her an asni.

She sipped happily and said: 'I think now you have paid for your vodkas.'

'Are you hungry?'

'I am always hungry. That is one of my troubles.' She took a sip of her asni and half of it disappeared.

'Shall we have dinner here?'

'If it pleases you. I think you should try one of our national dishes. It is called *hakarl*.'

'Is it good?'

'We think so. But sometimes foreigners do not agree. It is shark that has been buried under the earth for a while. It is a little rotten and has a sort of rind round the outside.'

'I think perhaps I'll give it a miss this time,' I said.

We headed for the restaurant upstairs. It was big, the ceiling supported by pillars, with a dance floor in the middle, two bars and a small happy orchestra. Women and girls and a few men stood near the bars waiting for a happening.

Gudrun examined the menu and suggested that I try boiled sheep's head. I resisted and we both had sweet soup and mutton. I ordered a bottle of wine and a glass of beer for myself.

Gudrun regarded the beer with scorn. 'Pilsner,' she said. 'Water. The Government does not allow much alcohol in the beer – they think it will encourage drunkenness.'

'So everyone drinks vodka and brandy instead?'

'That's right,' she said, brightly.

'I never did understand politics.'

'Shall we dance?'

'Before we've eaten?'

But she was already on her feet, hand outstretched, waiting or commanding. She was wearing a dark blue evening skirt and a white silk blouse cut very low.

For a girl of her build she was lively on the floor. The music was Beatles or Rolling Stones or something like that, played and sung with vigour. She swung her arms around with abandon, laughed, sang a little and trod on a tourist.

Then we returned to our sweet soup. She drank this quickly, panting a little from her exertions. Her face was flushed and pretty and her soft blonde hair was brushed into wings in front of her ears so that it looked like a helmet.

I drank my beer which was not dissimilar from water and said: '*Skal*.'

'*Skal*,' she said. We looked into each other's eyes in search of messages.

'I'm enjoying myself,' I said.

'That is good. In Iceland we know how to enjoy ourselves.' She then embarked on the cross-examination which swiftly follows any meeting between man and woman in any country; although in most other countries it is often conducted with subtlety.

Gudrun said: 'Are you married?' Elsewhere they favour an exploratory, 'I suppose you had to leave your wife in England?'

'No,' I said.

'Are you divorced?'

'Yes.'

'It is best.'

'What do you mean – it is best?'

'If two people do not get on then they should part.'

'And if there are children?' Not that I had any.

'Then they should still part because they will only make the children unhappy.' She drank some wine and attacked the mutton. 'In Iceland we love children but we do not let them rule our lives. In any case many are born before marriage – thirty-three per cent I believe.'

'And then the couples marry?'

'Very often.' She warmed to her subject. 'I am travelling a lot and I do not understand your ways in other countries. There is so much talk about this permitting society.'

'Permissive,' I said.

'We have always been like that in Iceland – but we do not talk about it all the time. If a man and a woman are attracted to each other then they should make the love. But why make big fusses about it all the time?'

I imagined that her Icelandic philosophy was immensely popular in the Skyways Hotel at London airport – or wherever Icelandair overnighted.

'Do *you* have any children?'

'Only one,' she said, and popped the last piece of mutton into her mouth.

'Does the child live with you?'

'Oh no,' she said. 'He is away.' She patted her lips with a napkin. 'You will perhaps see him.'

Beside our table a girl of about sixteen was dancing with a partner two or three years older. Her face was very pale and she did not look well. Her hair was long and honey-coloured, parted in the centre, and her eyes were dark and staring. In London she would have been part of Chelsea, on the brink of debbiness, embarking on a few years of hunt balls and pot before marrying into stockbroking. Her partner wore a dark flared jacket, light grey trousers and a flowered blue shirt; his hair was blond, almost yellow, and his eyes very blue.

Gudrun said. 'What are you staring at?'

'Just that couple. They're rather striking.'

'Just two young Icelanders enjoying themselves.' She pointed towards the bar at the entrance to the restaurant. 'See those two men there?'

'Which two?' Icelandic men had now begun to appear and were standing around, drinks in their hands, apparently waiting to be chosen, like the girls in the dance halls of my youth.

'Those two in the front looking around the restaurant.'

One was middle-aged, balding, wearing a brown gaberdine suit, square-toed shoes and a button-down collar. The other was slighter, fair, sharp.

'Who are they?'

'Police,' she said. 'American and Icelandic. It has gone ten and all Americans must be back at their base. That is the agreement that the Americans have with our Government except on Wednesdays when there is no drink sold in

Reykjavik. Those two policemen are looking for Americans breaking the rules. If they catch any they will be in the big trouble.'

The Icelandic plain-clothes man stared at me and spoke to the American in the brown suit. The American appraised me, shook his head and continued examining the dancers. I followed his gaze. The girl with the pale face and dark eyes was still dancing, staring across the heads of the diners. But of her partner there was no sign.

We danced and drank till midnight. Then Gudrun said we should leave. I went to the toilet and found several Icelandic men gathered there with their drinks – escaping briefly from a predominantly female gathering. They were talking about politics, fishing and their expectations for the night.

Outside the hotel a crowd was still clamouring to get in. Gudrun led me to her baby Fiat and we drove to her apartment on the east side of the city.

The apartment was smart and untidy, adorned and littered with the paraphernalia of a stewardess. Ornaments from foreign parts, duty-free packets of cigarettes, an airline bag, half-consumed bottles of whisky and gin, a framed photograph of Gudrun with some air-crew grinning muzzily over champagne glasses.

'I hope that was after a flight,' I said.

'Of course,' she said. She looked at them fondly. 'Vonderful men.' She poured me a large Scotch and retired to the bathroom where she made a lot of noise with water.

I stood at the window of the apartment and gazed across the sea to the mountains. The 1 a.m. light was mauvish and the crumpled peaks were sugared with new snow even though it was June.

The apartment was on the fifth floor of a skyscraper block in an area known as 'Snob Hill' because of the expensive villas there. From the bathroom there came the faint smell of Hydrogen Sulphide as Gudrun washed herself in the hot water piped from natural springs.

I was wondering whether to start undressing when she reappeared – naked. She stood in front of me and said: 'You like me?'

I pulled the curtains and said: 'Yes.'

'Then you must get undressed.' She took off my jacket and tie with deft movements. 'And now I will wait for you in bed.' She paused on the way to light a cigarette; her alpine breasts swung slightly; her buttocks jogged jauntily. Someone once said that the spectacle of a half-dressed woman was more erotic than the sight of a nude one: he was wrong.

We made love with enthusiasm, pleasure and – certainly in her case – expertise that might have aroused jealousies in my conformist soul if I had been more involved.

Then we smoked cigarettes and looked at the ceiling through the lacework of smoke.

She touched my face and said: 'You have very sensitive eyes.'

'I'm a very sensitive person.'

'Why did you divorce your wife?'

'I didn't – she divorced me.'

'Why?'

'She found someone else.'

'Then she was wery stupid,' Gudrun said.

'So was I.'

She raised herself on one elbow and examined me. 'You are a very interesting man.'

'Thanks,' I said. 'Brains first, then looks.'

She ignored me. 'You have a wery sensitive face and yet your ways and your body are hard.' She nibbled at her lower lip. 'What are your hobbies, Mr Conran?'

'Bill,' I said.

'What are your hobbies, Bill?'

'Bird watching.' I waited for the amusement that usually greeted the confession.

'Vonderful,' Gudrun said. 'We have the most vonderful birds in Iceland.'

'You can say that again.'

She looked puzzled and said: 'We have the most vonderful birds in Iceland.'

'I hope to see some of them before I leave.'

'When will you leave, Bill?'

'As soon as I've sorted out this eruption of yours.'

'When will you go and see Hekla?'

I would have to go soon, I thought, to maintain the cover. 'Tomorrow, maybe.'

'Then I shall take you.'

'Aren't you flying?'

'Not for two days. So, it is arranged. I have a friend who will lend me a Land Rover. I will pick you up at your guest-house. Or,' she added thoughtfully, 'you can stay here.'

'It might be better if you picked me up,' I said.

She lit another cigarette with a gold Dunhill lighter. 'Yesh,' she said, 'it might be better. Johann might come back in the morning.'

I digested this enigmatic information. 'Who is Johann and where might he be coming back from?'

'Johann is my boyfriend. He is out fishing at this moment. He is on a trawler.'

I imagined him at the door, enormous in a blue sweater and thigh-boots, delivering me a stunning blow as if I were an errant cod. 'Is he the father of your child?' It sounded unbelievably pompous.

She looked surprised. *'Gud minn almattugur'* – which means Good Lord – 'he is not. He is just a boyfriend but he likes me very much and he comes round here straight from his ship.'

I glanced at my watch; it was 2.30 a.m. 'What time does his ship get back?'

'I do not know. When they have enough fish.' She shrugged and dismissed the ardent, salty Johann from the conversation. 'So, it is fixed – I will pick you up tomorrow at six in the evening. It is best to see Hekla at night when at least there is a little dusk.'

'Fine,' I said. 'There's just one thing.'

'And that is?'

'Don't bring Johann.'

She smiled and shifted her body so that her nipples touched my face. '*Elskan min*,' she said, which means darling. I noted that with familiarity she lapsed more into Icelandic. The breasts lowered fractionally and my powers of observation faded for a while.

Later she said: 'This eruption – is that your only reason for visiting Iceland?'

'Of course,' I said.

I washed in the sulphurous water and dressed. Outside the sky was icy bright. I kissed her and said: 'See you today – *blessadur*.'

She stood at the door, still naked, and said: '*Bles*.'

I walked back through the shopping centre of Laugavegur and down the hill to Laekjargata, the home of many Government offices, on the perimeter of the old city centre. At first there were a few teenagers around, a few drunks, a lot of broken glass – Icelanders are dedicated breakers of bottles.

Gradually I became aware of more activity. Police cars, policemen, an American military patrol.

I was stopped by a black-uniformed policeman. 'Your identification papers, please,' he said.

'What the hell's going on?'

'A girl has been found dead,' he said. 'We think she may have been murdered.'

Intuitively I knew that the dead girl was the girl with the long hair and dark wide eyes that I had seen dancing at the Saga.

6

Ruffled Feathers

The problem was how to get to know the suspects without arousing their suspicions. Laxdal was the easiest. I could charter one of his aircraft to fly around Hekla and I could offer good money. For really good money Valdimar Laxdal would fly *into* one of the craters . . .

A friendship could probably be arranged with Hafstein through the freemasonry of ornithology. We bird watchers were a formidable alliance. He was an anti-social man. But a sighting of one of the ten breeding pairs of white-tailed eagle left in Iceland would socialise the most diffident of ornithologists – even if it were fictitious.

The most difficult was Magnusson, the trawler-owner. There was no common ground there. In fact Magnusson might be hostile following his role in the Cod War of 1958-59 when British and Icelandic ships clashed over fishing limits around the island. Sigurdson would have to find a solution to that one.

I rose at nine, had a sulphurous shower and breakfasted upstairs with my landlady and some delegates to a marine conference. They came from Florida, the Philippines, Brazil

and South Africa and they all listened with patience and
little comprehension to her views on the younger generation
and strong drink. The Brazilian looked particularly hungover,
I thought.

It was a rainbow morning with showers and sunshine
competing. The newspapers were full of the girl's death:
murders of any kind were a rarity in Iceland.

I called at Sigurdson's office in the eastern part of town.
The office was clinically clean, incongruous for a man not
notably tidy in his appearance.

'*Komdu sael*,' he said. 'Sit down, my friend. Have some
coffee.' The omnipresent jug was on the table and he called
for another cup. 'A brandy, perhaps, to go with it?'

'No thanks, I'm still recovering from my first encounter
with you.'

He poured coffee with a steady hand. 'That was a good
night, eh? We drink much. We must do it again and we
must find some girls.' The faded eyes searched my face. 'Or
perhaps you have found one already?'

I ignored the bait. 'Anything on that bullet that was
intended to put a hole in my head?'

'Not yet. Today perhaps. But I don't think it will help us.
A British bullet, a German bullet, a Russian bullet. So what
will that tell us?'

I sipped the excellent coffee, black and sweet and strong.
'Do you have a lead on the murder of this girl?'

The beam left his pale face and he fingered the round
scar on his neck. 'That is a terrible thing. Never before have
we had anything like that in Iceland.'

'But do you have a lead?'

'It is not my business. It has nothing to do with spies.'

'Was she raped?'

'I told you – it has nothing to do with me.'

'But you must have heard.' I sensed uncharacteristic
reticence.

'It is apparently difficult to tell. The girl was experienced, it seems. There is a possibility that intercourse may have taken place and a suggestion that it may have been against her will. The pathologist has not yet established the cause of death.'

'Can I see the body?'

'Whatever for?' He sat back, fists white-knuckled on the desk; I didn't think I should like to be interrogated by Einar Sigurdson.

'I think I might be able to help your investigating officers. Was the girl at the Saga last night?'

He relaxed a little. 'So were you, my friend – or so I have been told.'

'You had me under surveillance? That wasn't very trusting of you, Einar.'

He smiled, much more happy now. 'You were seen there with a very attractive young lady. Reykjavik is a small place, Herra Conran. I presume that you believe you know who the dead girl was and you saw her with someone?'

'Something like that. Just an instinct, really.'

'In this game instincts are everything,' Sigurdson said, as if he were lecturing a class of police recruits. 'If you really want to see the body then I can arrange it.'

We went to the morgue together. Her eyes were closed and there was a bruise on her bloodless lips. Her long hair had been drawn behind her and she looked like a child.

'She was seventeen,' Sigurdson said.

I gave him a description of the boy she had been with to pass on to the detectives.

Sigurdson made a few notes and said: 'The trouble is that she was with many boys that night.'

'You mean physically?'

'Not physically. Just drinking and dancing. I expect they already have a description of the boy you saw.'

We returned to his office and drank more coffee. It was my turn to be interrogator. 'You seem to know more about this case than you indicated at first.'

'I told you the truth, my friend – it is none of my business. Nor is it any of yours. The two of us are in this office at this moment to break a spy ring. Is that not so?'

It was so. But I was uneasy about his attitude.

He picked the dossiers on the three suspects that I had brought back. 'What do you think of our three friends?'

'Not much,' I said. 'There's not much to go on.'

'Has it occurred to you that one or two or even all three of them might not be Icelandic? It is quite possible. The Russians plan a long way ahead – as the West has found out to its cost.'

'I find it a little hard to believe.'

He shrugged as if to say, 'These Russians'. He emptied the coffee jug into his own cup. 'What are you going to do now?'

'See Laxdal, I think. Then go over Hafstein's place in the country while he's at work.'

'Make sure you don't alarm them.'

'It's a risk I'll have to take. I'm going to hire a plane from Laxdal. I shall want your help in bugging the homes and offices of all three of them.'

'All right, my friend. But be careful.' He paused. 'Soon you will have to go and see Hekla from the ground other-wise people will begin to wonder how you are carrying out your research.'

'I'm going this evening,' I said.

'By yourself?'

'Not by myself.'

He rose and squeezed my hand very hard. 'Good hunting,' he said. 'But remember – Reykjavik is a very small place.'

I left him in his tidy office paring his fingernails with a

paper cutter and walked up past the lake to the city airport where Valdimar Laxdal ran his business – whatever that really was.

Valdimar Laxdal's office was inside a hangar owned by Loftleidir, Iceland's other international airline. It contained a desk, a worn aircraft tyre, a tailplane, three crates of aircraft parts from London, two bosomy calendars and an electric light without a shade. It smelled of kerosene and coffee. Laxdal smelled of powerful aftershave. He was fair and tanned, which was unusual in Iceland – I imagined he used an ultraviolet lamp. He was older than his photograph, a man probably taking many precautions to slow down the ageing process. Exercise, dieting, cutting down on liquor, importing hormone pills from Europe.

His face was thin, the chin dimpled. 'Dimpled chin, the devil within.' His cheeks shone from a close shave, his eyes were grey with pinpoint pupils, his hair was razor-cut. A hard and dangerous man, attractive to women – a fervent admirer of Valdimar Laxdal.

He sauntered in, twirling expensive French sunglasses in his hand. He wore white overalls and for one illusory moment I saw him at a bedside with a stethoscope hanging from his neck: he would have enjoyed the illusion.

'Good morning,' he said. 'What can I do for you?' This time the accent was English, not American. And the English was very good – just a little mannered.

'I'd like to hire one of your aircraft,' I said.

'Are you a pilot?'

'No. I want you to fly me as close as possible to Hekla.'

'Are you a photographer?'

'No.' I told him what I was supposed to be.

'It is very dangerous to get too close.'

'I'm not asking you to get too close.' I lit a cigarette and offered him one. He shook his head: smoking contributed to ageing. 'Just close enough. There is a lot of controversy about the eruptions. One school of thought says they are not genuine Hekla eruptions because the Hekla eruptive rift runs from north-northeast to south-southwest and these craters run north to south.'

'And the other school of thought?' He leaned back in his chair, fingertips pressed together.

'The other school of thought derives from lava analysis. You have probably heard of the geo-chemist Gudmunder Sigvaldson?'

'I have heard of him.'

'According to him the samples had a very high acid content at the beginning of the eruption. This decreased later. This is typical of Hekla eruptions.'

Even if you don't believe me, I thought, you've got to admit that I've done my homework.

'And what will flying near the craters achieve?'

A good question, Valdimar Laxdal. 'Their pattern is important,' I said. 'I believe that the initial strength of the eruptions prevented accurate assessment. I believe that those craters do lie north-northeast to south-southwest.'

But Laxdal had also done his homework. 'You could be right,' he said. 'Observation was difficult at the beginning. As you know, the height of the first eruptions was phenomenal according to radar at Keflavik.'

I nodded profoundly.

'It was very difficult and highly dangerous to get anywhere near them,' he said.

'That's my point,' I said. I threw in a bit about the first earthquake measuring strength four on the Richter Scale.

He countered with a few statistics about the craters. A total of thirteen on the first day. Then he probed a bit more. 'What areas do you intend to concentrate upon when you're on the ground?'

'Certainly around the Burfell power plant where they

evacuated all the women and children. And, of course, some of the ash has fallen as far north as Hornbjarg.'

We regarded each other quietly. He said: 'It will still be dangerous to fly very close to the craters.'

'I'm aware of that,' I said.

'And it will therefore cost you more.'

'I'm willing to pay more. At least your government is.'

'Very well. When do you wish to fly?'

'The day after tomorrow – weather permitting.'

'Very well. Perhaps you would oblige me with a payment now. Half perhaps?' He gave me a conspiratorial smile – *let you and I cheat the government together*. 'We can perhaps reach an agreement together?'

'I don't quite know what you mean,' I said primly, and wondered if he was the man who had tried to kill me on the road from Keflavik.

The messenger arrived just in time – a breathless girl from the terminal building. 'There's a phone call for you, Mr Laxdal,' she said. 'They say it's very urgent Something about some money.'

'In the terminal building?'

She nodded breathlessly.

'I'll try and take it here.' He picked up the receiver but it was dead: Sigurdson had done his job well.

Laxdal swore tersely in Icelandic. But money was money, an important commodity in his life. 'Please excuse me,' he said. 'I shan't be long.'

I watched him across the hangar floor with the girl. Then I unscrewed the base of the telephone and inserted Martz 's bug, his insect, his nasty little eavesdropper, inside. I screwed the base on again and looked out across the hangar. No sign of Laxdal.

I went to his side of the desk and opened the drawer. Maps, bills, aerial photographs of Reykjavik. A razor, a pencil sharpener, a grease pencil, a copy of *Playboy*. Nothing incriminating, nothing surprising.

I flipped through the *Playboy* and a photograph of Gudrun fell on to the floor.

When he returned he was taut with suppressed anger. Monosyllabic, the knife half out of the sheath of cultivated behaviour.

'A profitable trip?'

'It was a mistake.' He glared at me as if it were my fault, which it was. He picked up the receiver: it was working. He swore again and I hoped that Sigurdson's monitor was not a man of delicate sensibilities.

'I'm sorry,' I said.

'So it is fixed – we fly the day after tomorrow?'

'It is fixed.'

I got up to go.

'Mr Conran – or is it Professor Conran?'

'Just plain mister.'

'Haven't you forgotten something?'

'Ah, the money.' I handed him a thin wad of kronur. He took it and began to count it. It was too much – but it was money well spent.

Hveragerdi is a small wandering place with 768 inhabitants, many hot springs, a geyser which erupts frequently and a profusion of hothouses. The hothouses are heated by natural steam, and tomatoes, bananas and grapes prosper in its warmth.

When you walk around the village you come across patches of soft, smoking earth. Elsewhere steam jets savagely from bore-holes.

I parked the Chevrolet outside the Hotel Hveragerdi and tried to look like a tourist with my camera and guidebook. In most other places in the world you would choose the hours of darkness if you were contemplating a break-in; in Iceland in the summer this is impossible. Luckily Hafstein's house was on the outskirts of the village and was partially screened by a jet of steam.

It was neat and white like the rest of Hveragerdi, with a green corrugated iron roof and a hothouse full of tomatoes. A pipe led away from the hothouse towards the crumpled hills where Hafstein presumably had a private source of steam.

I picked the lock of the back door, let myself into the kitchen and stood for a moment listening to the house. A creak of wood, an electrical click in the refrigerator, a clock ticking, a tap dripping. Outside steam rolled past the window and the smell of sulphur was strong in the air.

I went into the living room. A bachelor place with a television set as a substitute for – friend or enemy. Modern furniture, multiple-store carpet, a seascape and a green Chinese face print on the walls – the essentials, unloved, bought during one excursion into town.

But I had not reached the shy soul of Emil Hafstein. Beside the television there was a door, locked; but not with intent to discourage burglars because I opened it in less than a minute.

From the walls of the study birds stared at and through me with disdain. Glassy, dusty, frozen savagery. From inland a white-tailed eagle, a gyrfalcon, old *Nyctea scandiaca* the snowy owl; from the cliffs and waves a petrel, a fulmar, a kittiwake and the sad parrot-clown puffin; from Lake Myvatn, a Barrow's goldeneye, a harlequin and a scaup.

Now I was close to Hafstein. Knowing him better than I would if I had met him. And ashamed of it because it was like reading someone's diary. If man had any right to anything then surely it was a sanctuary – beneath the sea, in the skies, in attic, study, studio or cobwebbed potting shed – the private confessional for braggart, pervert, introvert. And I had intruded, as brutally as a drunk in a convent.

On an easel in the corner stood a half-finished painting of a church and beside it a book with a photograph of the same church. The caption said: '*Old Roman Catholic Church situate adjacent mud pools and hot spring, one km from Hveragerdi. Now disused.*' The author did not seem to have much feeling for old disused Roman Catholic churches. The painting was being executed with loving, amateurish strokes.

The desk was covered with peeling, moss-green leather scrolled with gold-leaf. The mess of papers was weighted here and there with chunks of ancient lava. I ducked the gaze of the birds and opened the drawer of the desk. There was a photograph of a girl inside; she was wearing a picture hat and a summer frock of immediate post-war length; she was smiling self-consciously at the camera and at the bottom she had written 'To Emil with Love', which I imagined was tantamount to an avowal of lifelong devotion from such a girl. Dead? Discarded? The answer, perhaps, to Hafstein's lonely ways.

Under the photograph was a file bound with pink ribbon. The network, the contacts, the pick-up points . . . I opened the file and began to read a thesis on the migratory habits of *Calidris canutus*, called the *bjartmafur* in Icelandic and the knot in English. Hafstein had been observing it in the Westman Isles. If the stuffed puffin had been alive to sense my suspicions he would have died laughing or laid an egg.

I slipped one bugging device behind the snowy owl and another under the telephone in the living room.

The quiet was brooding and heavy. Just the small sounds of a house breathing. And then the crunch of a foot on the black ash outside. Or was it my imagination? The cumulus of steam thinned briefly and I fancied I saw a face.

I withdrew to the study and waited there with the birds and my Smith & Wesson. Five minutes, no further sound.

I read the thesis, exhaustive and accomplished. I read the other papers, searched his books and middle-aged bachelor clothes, looked for wall-safes or hidden spring drawers. Nothing. A man of austere, listless habits away from his birds and churches; his only indulgence seemed to be sweets, an indulgence shared by many Icelanders.

Hafstein's loneliness settled around me; it seemed inconceivable that he could be a spy, a traitor, a Marxist or even a shop-steward of the local stuffed-bird society.

I closed the drawer, smoothed the owl's ruffled feathers, avoided the glare of the gyrfalcon and let myself out of Emil Hafstein's sanctuary of innocent pleasure.

I was across the lounge and three steps into the kitchen when the barrel of the pistol was rammed in my spine.

I swung and ducked in one movement, chopping upwards with the side of my left hand. But I wasn't playing games with an amateur. He clipped me quite gently on the mastoid and I lost consciousness.

7

Hekla

Half an hour later I blessed the professionalism. The swelling was small, the pain sharp but curable. I lay on the kitchen floor for a while, then lumbered around the house checking to see if my little insects were still alive and safe: they were.

I let myself out and walked through the mushrooms of steam to the hotel and phoned Gudrun. She was due to pick me up at 6 p.m. in Reykjavik; I told her to come on out to Hveragerdi, which is on the way to Hekla, and to bring some painkillers and my sheepskin coat with her. Then I went into the hotel and ordered a brandy.

'What happened?' Gudrun asked. Her concern warmed me as much as the brandy.

'I fell climbing one of those bloody hills.'

She frowned. 'What were you doing here and why were you climbing hills?'

'I'm writing a paper on the knot,' I said. 'That's the sort of terrain you would find them in.' I hoped she knew nothing whatsoever about ornithology.

'What's a knot?'

'The *bjartmafur*.'

She nodded vaguely. 'Are you fit enough to go to Hekla?'

'I'm all right,' I said.

She drove the Land Rover well, talking a lot and pointing out rivers, mountains and farmhouses wedged into the flanks of senile volcanoes.

'It was in farms like those that they wrote the sagas,' she said. 'Vonderful men like our own Snorri Sturluson.'

'A sleepy sort of name.'

She ignored me. 'You see we have no trees hardly to speak of?'

I nodded and a jab of pain passed from one ear to the other.

'Ari the Learned said that Iceland once had the trees but they were all cut down to make fires. But there are still a few birch in the east.'

It was to be a guided tour and nothing would deter her. I made the occasional contribution. I pointed at the lava field on either side of us – frozen waves covered with verdigris. 'Do you know the names of the moss beginning to grow on the lava?'

She shook her head irritably.

'*Rhacomitrium lanuginosum* and *rhacomitrium canescens*.' I had practised the pronunciation on the underground taking me home to Kensington and I was rather proud of it. 'You can tell the age of the lava from the vegetation. When it gets a bit older you get small shrubs and later on birch.'

Ari the Learned apparently had nothing to contribute to this.

We passed some more patches of smoking earth and a fine wide river combed by boulders into white tresses. Then we began to climb and I saw the first far-flung black ashes of Hekla. She stopped the Land Rover and I filled a bag with the ash which was like coke. The land had been pasture; now it was a black wilderness.

'Katla is also a wonderful volcano,' Gudrun said. 'It is

covered by a glacier which melts when it erupts causing huge floods and explosions, and storms of ash that turn day into night.'

I recalled the description from a guide book. 'Very soon you'll be telling me that Iceland is Greenland and Greenland is Iceland.'

'That is right,' she said. 'We have the good climate here. Especially in the south. You should have come last week for the sunshine.

'Or later in the year?'

'Or later in the year.'

'That's what they all say,' I said.

'Your head is hurting you,' she said.

'How was Johann?' I asked.

'Ah, Johann. He did not come. He must still be looking for the fish.' She let out the clutch and we continued climbing. 'Perhaps he has found another girl.'

'Would you mind if he had?'

'No.' She paused and added: 'Not now.'

She wore a pale blue headscarf, corduroy jeans, sealskin boots and a dark blue anorak unzipped at the front to reveal a powder-blue jersey that was far too small for her.

'Are things so different now?' I asked.

'Yesh,' she said.

'I saw a photograph of you today.'

'It is good, is it not?'

'I didn't look too carefully.'

'It took all day that photograph. He took many, many pictures.'

'It didn't look all that good,' I said.

'You mean the picture for Icelandair?'

'No, not that one.' I lit a cigarette carefully, surprised at my reluctance to ask the positive question.

'Which is this photograph then?'

'I went to Valdimar Laxdal's office today. I wanted to

charter one of his aircraft to fly over Hekla. When he opened his desk there was a photograph of you in the drawer.' I made a production of inhaling, exhaling, examining the tip of the cigarette. 'Did you know him well?'

She seemed nonplussed for the first time since I met her. She took my cigarette and drew on it. We passed an extinct volcano crater filled with milky blue water; ahead the skyline of peaks was wrapped in scarves of mist. The track was muddy and deeply-rutted and some of the scoria tossed fifteen miles distance from Hekla was as big as rocks.

'Well, did you?'

'I knew him.' Her mittened hands held the wheel very firmly.

'Intimately but not well.'

'I think that is some sort of joke. I do not like those sort of jokes.' The tyres crunched on the ash as she swung off the track to avoid a mire of wheel-tracks. 'Very well, we were lovers.'

'Does that mean you loved him?'

'Yes, I think perhaps I did then.' She turned to the defence of her country's morals. 'But that is not why I slept with him. I would have slept with him anyway if he had asked. He is an attractive man and we were attracted to each other. Therefore it is natural that we make love. That is the way it is in Iceland.' She brightened a little. 'We eat we drink, we make the jokes, we make love. That is how it was intended. We think that you in England and America are the ones without morals. Why is it wrong to make love?'

'I didn't say it was.'

'Already we are getting too serious.'

'I agree,' I said.

This seemed to annoy her. 'You make me serious because I know how you English and Americans are about these things. If I were with an Iceland man I would not have to explain.'

'Do you still go with him?'

'We are no longer lovers.'

'Did he go back to his wife?'

'He never left his wife.'

The situation sounded more international than exclusively Icelandic. 'Is he the father of your child?' Jesus, I thought, get me another script writer.

'Yes,' she said. The tyres spat lava as we accelerated round a hairpin bend.

I heard Hekla about four miles before we reached it. A continuous grumble of distant thunder becoming louder and sharper as we got nearer. We parked the Land Rover on a ledge overlooking a plain. It was midnight, and the white peaks of the mountains on the far side of the plain floated on mauve mist in the uncertain light. Immediately below flowed a wide river of lava, dark and embedded with red jewels: to the right, around a jutting crag, stood the craters.

Smoke was suspended high above, being pushed around by the jets of hot air as docilely as jellyfish in strong currents. I took Gudrun's hand because we were children in the presence of all this and we climbed down the hill to the plain. Half way down we saw the great mouth of Hekla spewing molten earth into the sky. The red lava, the burning earth, sprayed up like storm waves hitting a jetty; with a regular rhythm – the pulse of the world. The noise was a continuous artillery barrage, the crust of the earth felt very fragile under our feet.

On the plain we stood within a couple of feet of the lava. A wall of grey coke ten feet high, half a mile wide, carrying red caves and chasms with it on its inexorable journey. Every second or so a segment fell from the top in front of the base: that was how it advanced. All the time it grumbled and muttered as it flexed its clinker muscles.

We skirted its path and walked towards the craters. There was hardly any ash now and the dark tough ground was embroidered with mauve flowers.

Sightseers heading for the craters were scattered across the plain. The daring got to within about three quarters of a mile of them with their cameras and binoculars and sandwiches.

We walked in silence, jumping small ravines, pausing to look back at the lava, grey and smoking where it had cooled: a World War One battlefield with silhouetted lava shapes like shattered farmhouses and tree stumps.

We stopped about a mile from the craters and rested. Gudrun produced bread and cheese which we ate at the ringside and forgot insignificant human behaviour. I wondered how you started a conversation in front of the Gates of Hell.

The problem was solved for me. A voice behind said: 'Hallo, Conran old man. Fancy meeting you here.'

The triteness of the remark in such majestic surroundings suited Jefferey.

I introduced Gudrun and he looked at her as if she were by now in possession of all Iceland's NATO secrets.

He picked up my camera and said: 'Will we be getting any photographs through the post this time?'

You might well be getting a fist in your mouth, I thought. 'Perhaps,' I said. 'You never know your luck. I know you enjoyed the previous consignment. Did you get a good price for them in Soho? No difficulty with customs I suppose – diplomatic privilege and all that.'

He looked pointedly at Gudrun. *'Malheur ne vient jamais seul.'* He sat down, immaculate for the occasion in climbing gear, trousers tucked into knee-high woollen socks, and heavy boots. His black hair looked as if it had just been combed, glossy with the usual wave slipping down his forehead. He was a living anachronism and he would go far in the British diplomatic service. Or would he?

'How did you manage to get posted to Iceland?' I asked.

'It just happened, old man. You know how the F.O. is.'

'Bit of a come-down, isn't it?'

'Not really,' he said. 'I'm just in transit, really. Something rather cush lined up for me in South America. Or so I hear on the old grapevine.' He looked at Gudrun's bosom with passionate interest which, with a British diplomat, is denoted by a tautening of one nostril.

Gudrun said: 'What do you think of our volcano, Mr Jefferey?'

'Absolutely marvellous,' Jefferey said, his eyes still X-raying her jersey.

She zipped up her anorak.

'I think we'll be moving off,' I said.

'Do you mind if I stroll along with you?'

'No,' I said. We both knew that I lied.

The explosions became louder and the red spume leapt higher into the sky. I photographed it all and we returned past the smoking battlefield towards the Land Rover.

'So you're a stewardess,' Jefferey said brilliantly.

Gudrun said 'Yes' because there really wasn't anything else to say.

'Damned interesting job that.'

'Yes,' she said. 'And what do you do, Mr Jefferey?'

'This and that,' he said. 'Help H.E. out when he's a bit pushed.'

She frowned. 'Who is this H.E.?'

'The British Ambassador,' Jefferey said.

'What a funny name,' she said. 'It sounds almost Japanese.'

As we neared the Land Rover and the river of lava was far below us Jefferey said: 'Could I have a word in your ear, old man?'

'Does it have to be now?'

'No time like the present.'

'Could you wait in the Land Rover a minute,' I said to Gudrun. 'Mr Jefferey wants to tell me a dirty joke.'

She looked at us as if we were a couple of queers.

I rounded on Jefferey and said: 'Look here you bloody little amateur. Do you realise you could balls the whole thing up carrying on like this in front of an Icelandic girl? I'm supposed to be studying the fall-out from this bloody volcano and you start acting like a police informer.'

Jefferey was imperturbable. 'Don't blow your top, old man. It's just that H.E. is a bit worried about your performance.'

'You mean that Japanese gentleman?'

Jefferey brushed aside unwelcome words like crumbs from his waistcoat. 'He knows about Moscow . . .'

'Because you told him.'

'A lot of people know about your behaviour in Moscow. I don't know why you harbour such a grudge – I think we treated you rather decently.'

'Carry on,' I said. 'What is upsetting the Ambassador? I presume he doesn't want any British involvement.'

'Can you blame him?'

'I understood that Britain was a member of NATO.'

The crumbs were brushed aside again. 'The point is, old man, that as soon as you chaps get into trouble you come dashing round to us for help. We don't want you coming round to us here in Iceland. Our relations with the Icelandic Government are very good now. We don't want any scandal.'

'And why do you think there should be any?'

He tucked an errant fold of trouser into his socks and patted the wave over his forehead as he straightened up. 'You did spend the night with this girl after you'd been to the Saga . . .'

'My word,' I said, 'Iceland is a small place.' I lit a cigarette and flicked the smoking match over the cliffs towards the lava below. 'But jealousy will get you nowhere, Jefferey.'

The crumbs were brushed aside with less nonchalance. 'The trouble is, Conran, you can't go to bed with a girl without arranging worldwide distribution of the consummation.'

'What did you do with those photographs, Jefferey? Use them as an aphrodisiac for some of those little secretary birds after a candlelit dinner for two in your apartment?'

The imperturbability was now glacial hatred. 'Just don't involve the Embassy with any of your squalid behaviour. It's just possible that we wouldn't help you this time.'

'Oh yes you would,' I said. 'Don't kid yourself, Jefferey. And by the way, old man, I suggest you sack the amateur sleuth who followed me from the Saga. He fell asleep on the job because I didn't stay the night.'

'I'm sure you stayed long enough for photographs to be taken.'

I turned and walked towards the Land Rover where Gudrun was beginning to show signs of impatience. I said: 'Will you please take a message back to H.E. for me, old man?'

'Not if it's facetious.'

I drew upon the centuries of breeding that had given us Conrans such an enviable reputation for wit and cultivated conversation. 'Tell him to get stuffed,' I said.

'I do not like that man,' Gudrun said.

'We have something more in common, then.'

'Where did you meet him?'

'In Moscow. I was helping the Russians with river pollution.' The lies tumbled out quite cheerfully.

'What was all that about photographs?'

'Just a joke. I took some pictures of British diplomats outside the Kremlin. I promised to send them through the post but I forgot.'

She parked the Land Rover in the street and we went up to her apartment. My head was aching again and my mouth felt as if I had been chewing lava.

'You look wery, wery tired,' she said. We sat on the sofa and she cradled my head against her.

'I feel very tired,' I said.

'I think you should stay here tonight.'

'What about Johann?' All I needed was a thump on my mastoid from an angry trawlerman.

'I think he is still looking for the fish.'

'I hope you're right.' Sleep was seeping through my body. 'I hope you're right.' I just managed to get my clothes off. Then I was asleep, my face content against her warmth.

8

Two Devious Policemen

By midday next day it was generally believed in Reykjavik that the dead girl had been raped and murdered by an American serviceman.

I met Sigurdson in a bar above a restaurant called the Naust where everyone drank long drinks made with spirits, and I drank a Pilsner. The bar was nautical in a yacht-club sort of way.

We sat at a table opposite each other, looked into each other's eyes and said '*Skal*'. Sigurdson shook his head and averted his gaze from the Pilsner, spiralled with gas bubbles.

'What did the pathologist's report on the girl say?' I asked.

Sigurdson drank deeply of his brandy and ginger ale. 'This thing need not concern you, Bill. We are together to catch spies, not to apprehend the man responsible for this unfortunate girl's death.'

The phraseology struck me as strange even for someone not fluent in English. 'Why do you say "responsible for the death of" instead of murdered?'

He sighed. 'My colleagues do not think she was murdered.'

'Look,' I said. 'Tell me what you know. I saw the girl alive, remember. And in the company of an Icelandic youth.'

'How do you know he was Icelandic?' 'He was very blond, blue-eyed . . .'

'So you presumed he was Icelandic. That is not very good police thinking. Did it not occur to you that there are many such Americans with Scandinavian or German ancestors?'

'All right then, so he could have been American. But I'm still interested. I saw them together. Don't you understand? Or hasn't your pathologist completed his report yet. Is that it, Einar? Are you ashamed of your colleagues' slowness?'

He finished his drink and said with ponderous dignity: 'We have one of the finest police forces in the world. We are only a little country but we are very modern. We could exist very well here without the Americans.'

'For God's sake let's not get on to that again. What does the pathologist say?'

'She had drunk a great deal and had vomited. We think she may have choked to death – asphyxia if you like. Her clothing was a little torn and there was a bruise on her lip. There was no evidence of recent sexual activity. Although she had had much experience for a girl of that age.'

'Then why is everyone in Reykjavik saying she was raped?'

'That was the first impression. It is very difficult to destroy. We presumed too much from the torn clothing.' He ordered another drink. 'We in Iceland find this disgusting. Nothing like it has ever happened before.'

'And that's why people presume it must be an American?'

He nodded. 'Because an Icelandic man would never have to resort to rape.'

'But this girl wasn't raped.'

'My colleagues are putting out a statement to that effect but I doubt if anyone will believe it.'

'You mean they won't want to believe it. Or the

Communists won't want them to believe it because this is great stuff for their anti-American campaign.'

'I think they are ready to believe this against the Americans because they do not understand crimes of sex.'

'There hasn't been a crime of sex.' The beer with its plaintive spirals of bubbles tasted weak and sour and I ordered a Scotch. 'What's more, I don't think this thing *is* outside my field of investigation any more. It's being used to whip up anti-American feeling and that's just what the boys we're after are trying to do.'

'I think you're making a mistake, my friend. Why do you not concentrate on our three suspects?'

I felt the tenderness behind my ear. 'One of them is concentrating on me.'

'I think we should arrest Hafstein now because whoever hit you will have alerted him.'

'No. I'm not convinced that Hafstein is working with anyone. I think that my assailant had gone there to ferret around just like I had.' I redirected the conversation back to the girl. 'Are your colleagues questioning Icelandic men as well as Americans?'

'Of course. In fact they have not so far questioned any Americans. The Americans are doing that themselves.' He leaned back in his chair and accused all Western countries more powerful than Iceland. 'That is the way they always like to do things.'

'Why were you so cagey about all this yesterday, Einar? Was it because you knew that suspicion would fall on an American and you wanted any agitation to get well under way before it was nipped in the bud by the lack of evidence of rape?'

'It was just none of my business.' His pale eyes stared at me flatly. 'Nor yours. In any case the medical report was not complete.'

'Will there be agitation now, Einar? Demonstrations and marches?'

'Perhaps. You should not concern yourself with such things. You are here to catch Russian spies. Do your work and then we will go out and get drunk and get some girls.'

'I think you welcome anti-American demonstrations.'

'We are a little country. You cannot understand what it is like being occupied by foreigners.'

'You make me sick,' I said. 'If the Americans weren't here then the Russians would be and you would have been shipped off to Siberia by now.' I finished my Scotch in one angry gulp. 'Do you know how they execute people in Russia, Einar? They give them a choice: they either shoot them in the back or put them down a uranium mine where they die slowly from radioactive poisoning. Even then most people choose the mines because they think a miracle might happen on the way. But it never does, Einar, it never does.'

He shrugged. 'That sort of story does not concern me.' He crushed his cigarette and stood up to leave.

'Oh yes it does, Einar. You just think about it before you start organising another anti-American demonstration.'

I didn't look to see if the point had been taken. I went downstairs to my Chevrolet and drove to the NATO base at Keflavik.

The base was hopping. Land Rovers and jeeps bustled around the blocks and the gingery military policeman at the gate jumped around desperately in his glass cage peering at the drivers of incoming vehicles.

I parked the Chevrolet outside and went in. The Icelandic policeman smiled engagingly, shuffling his pack of cards at the same time. But the American recognised me and said: 'Who do you want to see, sir?'

'Commander Martz,' I said.

'I reckon he's pretty busy, sir. Do you have an appointment?'

'Tell him Bill Conran's coming in to see him.'

'Okay, sir.'

He answered the phone, taking the opportunity to take off his glasses and massage the bridge of his thin nose. Without his glasses he looked defenceless. He said: 'I can't speak now, Mike. Yeah, as I hear it he's being interrogated right now.' He put down the receiver.

'Who's being interrogated?'

He looked at me short-sightedly and unhappily. 'It's not for me to say, sir. I'll find out if Commander Martz can see you.'

Commander Martz could – with a reluctance that communicated itself over the telephone.

As I went out to the Chevrolet the military policeman was putting on his spectacles again and resuming his petulant authority.

Martz's complex of Nissen huts was crowded with officers and men, worrying, colliding, saluting, obeying orders at the double. Outside his office a guard stopped me and said: 'Commander Martz will see you in a minute, Mr Conran, sir.'

'What the hell's going on around here?'

'That's not for me to say, sir.'

Which it wasn't. Ten minutes and two cigarettes later I went in to see Charlie. He was in civilian clothes, harassed, tired, massaging his cropped hair a great deal. He smiled without enthusiasm, but at least he tried. He was a nice, civil guy, was Charlie Martz. 'Good to see you, Bill old buddy,' he lied. 'But I guess today isn't a great day for spy catching.'

'It's always a good day for spy catching,' I said. 'Aren't you interested in where I put those little bugs of yours?'

'I sure am. But not right now. Could we maybe meet for a beer tonight?'

'Are the Icelanders putting the squeeze on you, Charlie?'

He lit a cigarette with his big, wind-shielded lighter – one of his favourite delaying tactics while he thought. 'I guess you know all about that,' he said, hoping I would reveal how much I did know.

'Yes,' I said, 'I know all about that.'

A Boeing 727 screamed down the runway and climbed in to a polished blue sky at an alarming angle.

'One helluva bad business.' Charlie Martz strongly suspected that I didn't know all about it and wasn't going to enlighten me if he could help it. The conversation was going to be as devious as the exchanges with Sigurdson because Charlie Martz had his own set of motives for avoiding or even confusing issues. He was a policeman with a diplomat's reticence, a liaison officer contained by military regulations, an American in a foreign country resentful of unwarranted hostility, an extrovert trained to subdue his exuberance. You could understand Charlie Martz being devious.

'They seem to think an American killed the girl,' I said.

He relaxed, presuming that was all I knew. 'The Communists have put them up to it, the lousy bastards.' He grinned his old frank grin permitting a glimpse of the gold tooth. 'No, I'm afraid today I'm in liaison instead of security.'

Now was the time to let him have it. Now he was so relaxed and frank. I said: 'What about the man you've been interrogating?'

His chair jerked forward. 'Do they know about him in Reykjavik?'

'Not as far as I know. But it won't be long because you've got a lot of civilian personnel on this base, haven't you, Charlie?'

He stared ruefully at the young Charlie Martz on the photographs on the wall. 'You're right, I guess.'

'What can you tell me about him, Charlie?'

'I can't see that it's any of your Goddamn business. It's got nothing to do with catching Russian spies.'

'It's all part and parcel of the same thing, Charlie. It's all part of the bigger plot. You yourself said the Communists were putting the Icelanders up to it. All over the world they're pulling tricks like this.'

The phone rang and Martz snarled briefly into it – 'I told you not to put any calls through to me.' He returned to me. 'So – it's all part of a world pattern. You're right, of course. But what the hell can you do about it? You're here to catch spies, not rapists.'

'There was no rape. And I'd like to see the man you're holding. I might be able to help – I saw that girl with a young man the night she died. When your patrolman came in with his Icelandic sidekick the man vanished.'

'How does that help anything? The guy you saw her with was probably just one of her Icelandic boyfriends. You know something? As I hear it that girl could have accommodated the whole Goddamn base before lunch and then gone out to meet her lover.'

'I'd like to see him, Charlie.'

He looked at me gloomily through a veil of cigarette smoke. 'Well,' he said, 'if it will make you happy. I suppose it can't do any harm. Then will you go back to your little bugs and Einar Sigurdson and let me be a liaison officer just for today?'

'Okay, Charlie,' I said, 'it's a deal.'

'But do me one great big favour – don't tell Sigurdson or any of his pals that you've seen this guy or they'll start cabling the President of the United States that Charlie Martz has given a limey preferential treatment.'

We walked down a polished corridor populated with lounging sailors and airmen who snapped upright as Martz walked past. At the end of the corridor was a brown door with two guards outside.

Before we went in Martz said: 'Don't forget this man hasn't been charged with anything.'

'The Icelandic police will want him as soon as they hear that you've questioned him.'

'Then they can get screwed,' Martz said.

'I thought you had to hand over a serviceman if a civilian crime has been committed.'

'What crime? All we know is that there's a dead girl.'

'They'll soon think of a crime. Manslaughter maybe – or whatever the Icelandic equivalent is.'

'I wouldn't even describe the guy in this room as a suspect. He's just having difficulty accounting for his movements on Saturday night.'

'All right, Charlie,' I said. 'But you know, and I know, that you've got a lot of trouble ahead of you.'

He shrugged and opened the door. Sitting at a table and looking very frightened, was the fair-haired boy with the bright blue eyes who had been dancing with the dead girl.

9

Airman First Class Fred Shirey

His name was Fred Shirey, airman first class, and he came from Cleveland, Ohio. Of German extraction with a name change somewhere along the line, born in St Paul, Minnesota.

His eyes were just as blue as I remembered them being; his hair was flaxen and longish on top; his complexion baby pink; in fact his colouring was albino except for the sapphire eyes. Now his face was dirty from fear and fatigue. He was wearing a blue windcheater, grey crew-neck sweater and grey slacks.

He looked at me with new apprehension as if I had come to take him away from the small functional office furnished with a table, a couple of chairs and a green metal filing cabinet.

I appealed to Martz. 'Could we have it from the beginning?

Martz sighed. 'Okay, once more won't do any harm.' He turned to Shirey. 'All right, airman, begin at the beginning. This is Mr Conran from England. He's here to help you.'

Shirey looked at me suspiciously. How could an Englishman help an American in trouble in Iceland?

'I can't explain now,' I said, 'but Commander Martz is right – I may be able to help you. Can you tell me about Saturday, right from the moment you left the base?'

'Okay, sir.' He searched in the pocket of his blue wind-cheater for a cigarette; I gave him one of mine.

Shirey said he caught the bus into town in the afternoon, hung around the shops for a while, went for a coffee in the Café Trod in Austurstraeti where you could sometimes get fixed up without going to a dance at the Saga or Loftleidir.

'What do you mean by fixed-up?' I asked. 'Girls?'

'Not necessarily. You can meet young people there and maybe get invited to a party or something. As you know we have to be off the streets by ten so if you can get an invite to someone's home you're okay. The young people seem to like us.' He looked warily at Martz, one of the perpetrators of an Icelandic-American plot to stop fraternising.

Martz said: 'Just get on with the story, airman.'

Shirey said he met some young Icelandic men at the Trod; they drank coffee and talked for a couple of hours. Then some girls came along and they all invited him to a party.

'But you didn't go,' I said.

'I sure did.' His bright eyes stared at me. Hard face, baby face – both, perhaps, in different circumstances. 'But they reckoned there weren't enough girls to go round.' He almost smiled. 'In Iceland – can you imagine that? I didn't want any trouble by getting involved with one of their girls so I decided to go find one for myself. Two, maybe – one for one of the other spare guys at the party. It isn't difficult to pick up girls here.' He looked defensively at Martz. 'The girls here seem to like us. So, come to that, do the guys.'

Martz said: 'I didn't make the rules, Shirey.' And to me he recited one of his liaison statistics: 'We average sixteen marriages a year with Icelandic girls.'

'That doesn't sound much with 3,000 American servicemen stationed here,' I said.

Martz said: 'A thousand of those are married.' Which left 2,000 bachelors kicking their heels at Keflavik on a Saturday night separated from the available nubile girls of Reykjavik by thirty-five kilometres of ancient lava.

I gave Shirey another cigarette and asked him: 'Do you like being posted in Iceland?'

Martz said: 'Now see here . . .'

Shirey said: 'Sure, I like it.' The resilience of the German settler showed through. 'It's what you make it. A challenge, I guess. We get good leave in Europe and there's a lot of sport and entertainment on the base and skiing up in the north.'

'And dodging the patrols at night,' I said.

He shrugged and I heard him thinking: Not in front of an officer – but if you're on a manslaughter rap what the hell? 'And dodging the patrols,' he said. 'Wouldn't you, if you were treated like a juvenile delinquent or something? All most of the guys want to do is to make some friends outside the base.'

'Okay, Shirey,' Martz said. 'Get on with Saturday night. How come you were at the Saga if you also went to a party?'

'Like I said – I went to look for some girls. I went to the Saga early and had a couple of drinks at the bar. No one paid much attention to me. It's the colour of my hair, I guess. I get taken for an Icelander – that's why the patrols often miss me . . .' He paused. 'Although I've had to run for it a couple of times.'

'Get on with it, Shirey,' Martz said.

'So I'm sitting there drinking a bourbon when I get into conversation with a couple of Icelandic guys. They thought I was Icelandic. When they found I was American they became very friendly – like they all do. And I drank a few more bourbons – got a little high, I guess. Then this girl came up. She was pretty high, too. The two men knew her and introduced her. She said she liked American boys and would I dance with her? So I did.' He went on the defensive again. 'Is there any law against that?'

'None that I know of,' I said. 'So you had a dance. What then?'

'She seemed pretty sexy. You know how it is on a dance floor.' He examined Martz and myself and decided that we didn't. 'You know, rubbing herself around, leg in between mine – all that sort of thing.'

'So you thought you were on to a good thing,' Martz said.

'Sure I did. I don't go around grabbing it but when it's offered I don't refuse.'

'Then what happened?' I asked.

'I was working out where we could go when I looked up and saw the patrol. An American and an Icelander. The American looked as if he might have recognised me from the base. So I told the girl to wait for me while I hid out. One of the staff there knows me and sticks me away in a room when the patrol comes in. When I came back, she'd gone.'

'She stayed quite a while,' I said.

'How do you know, sir?'

'I was there,' I said. 'I can back up your story so far.'

He digested this information, nibbling away at his bottom lip, giving himself a chipmunk look. His teeth were very white and even. Finally he said: 'I appreciate that, sir.'

'But only so far,' I said. 'What happened then?'

'I went looking for her. She was back in the bar downstairs. She said did I want to go with her and I said yes I did. I knew she was drunk but I also knew she wasn't any innocent virgin or anything like that. So I said, "Okay, where can we go?" And she said she lived in an apartment across the way with her parents but they were away in Akureyri or some place. So she got her coat and we walked down some streets until we came to her parents' place.' His speech slowed down and he shivered as he remembered what it was all about. 'Christ,' he said, 'it's cold.'

I tried to relax him a bit. 'I'll check on the Chill Factor.'

'That only applies in the winter,' Martz said. 'What happened in the apartment?'

Shirey clenched his fists, trying to control the shivers of fear. 'We sat on a sofa and played around a bit. Petting, if you like. She wanted it.' He looked through us, remembering. 'She wanted it bad. But she was too Goddamn drunk. She was very pale and I remember thinking she was going to throw up. I thought, Jesus this isn't for me. I mean, I've had girls and everything, but never when they're that bad.'

'How old are you?' I asked.

'Nineteen,' he said. 'Why?'

'It doesn't matter,' I said. 'Carry on.'

Outside a jet of some sort came in to land. A whine, a scream and silence. Shirey looked for it out of the window. He looked a long way from home.

He went on: 'So I asked her if she was all right. She said she was. Then she started pulling at her clothes. But I'd lost interest by then and all I wanted was out. I felt sorry for her, though, so I tried to make her lie down and take it easy. But she just grabbed at me. I broke loose and got the hell out of it.'

'How was she when you left?' I asked.

'Okay. Drunk like I said. But she was sitting up looking at me.'

'And that's all you did?'

'And that's all I did, so help me.'

'How far did the petting go?'

He looked embarrassed despite his experienced words. 'Far enough. Not too far.' He searched in his pocket for a cigarette and I gave him another. 'What do you want, a blow by blow account? I didn't screw her if that's what you mean. I would have but she was too drunk. I don't go for that sort of scene.'

'Do you swear she was alive when you left her?'

'On the Bible. I had nothing to do with that girl's death. When I left her she was stoned. But, Jesus, I'm not the first guy to have walked out on a girl because she was stoned.' He thought for a moment. 'If anyone is responsible for that girl's death it's the guy who bought her all that hooch.' He turned to Martz. 'Can I go now, sir?'

Martz shook his head, but his voice was almost kindly. 'Not yet, son.'

'Why not, sir? I haven't committed any crime.' There was a break in his voice and the shivering started again. 'Not unless picking up a girl and leaving her when you find she's drunk is a crime.'

'It's a bit more complicated than that,' Martz said inadequately. He had a son a couple of years younger than Shirey.

'I don't think we've quite finished,' I said. 'You say you went to that party?'

'I sure did. After I left the girl's apartment I went to the address they had given me. It wasn't far away. I had a ball,' he added as if he might never have one again.

'Then the people at the party will be able to give you an alibi for the time you were there?'

'Sure they will.'

I said to Charlie Martz: 'Are the people at the party being checked out?'

He stared bleakly at the sky which was half way through one of its quick-changes, with small white clouds darkening and fusing. 'Not yet. Not at our request anyway. It would alert the Icelanders to the fact that we've been questioning one particular airman.'

Shirey moved his head around as if the muscles at the nape of his neck ached.

I said: 'They'll know soon enough anyway.'

'We'll wait till that happens,' Martz said with Service obstinacy.

'Why, when they're bound to find out anyway?'

Martz picked up the ringing phone. For a couple of minutes he did most of the listening, supplying the occasional affirmative, massaging the chopped stalks of his hair with the tips of his fingers. Finally he said: 'Tell them they'll have to wait.' He replaced the receiver gently and thoughtfully. Then he turned to the two of us and said: 'They've found out.'

'Do you think Shirey had anything to do with it?' Martz stood gazing at the photograph of Kennedy and himself; I wondered if the young Naval officer had known then what deviousness lay ahead of him.

'No more than he said he did.'

'Nor do I.' He sat down and swivelled around in his chair. 'But they're clamouring for him out there.' He pointed in the direction of Reykjavik. 'I guess we'll have to hand him over. They're pretty fair,' he added, excusing himself.

'Don't do it, Charlie,' I said. 'Not yet anyway.'

'I told you this was none of your business. Stick to spies and bird watching. You should have learned your lesson in Moscow.'

'That boy hasn't committed any crime,' I said. 'And you know it. You've just admitted it. If you hand him over he'll be crucified by the Communists. He'll get bad publicity and the story will reach the papers in Minnesota and Cleveland. You could ruin him.'

'I know all about that, Bill old buddy,' he said, seeking camaraderie again because he knew that he was in the wrong. 'But there's a whole lot more to it than that. The future relations between America and Iceland. The future of this base. In 1959 there were a couple of incidents. An

American woman was taken in for some driving offence or something and we refused to hand her over to the Icelandic authorities. Then there was some sort of balls-up when some Icelander was found inside the base and held at gun-point. As a result of all that the commanding officer was recalled to the States. At least, that's the story the way the Icelanders tell it.'

The phone went. Martz put one hand over the mouth-piece and said: 'It's the Admiral.' He spoke with respect but no servility. He finished by saying: 'I would be grateful, sir, if you would agree to a few delaying tactics. After all, as far as we can make out, no crime has been committed.' The voice at the other end jangled on for another minute. Then Martz said: 'Thank you very much, sir,' and hung up.

'You're a good man, Charlie Martz,' I said.

He shrugged. 'That boy down the end of the corridor didn't ask to join the Air Force. And he didn't ask to come to Iceland. Just like they don't ask to go to Vietnam. I just hope to Christ they don't start a demonstration. The Admiral wasn't too pleased about what they did to the TV equipment.'

I grinned. 'You're getting too soft for this job, Charlie Martz.'

'Screw you,' he said. 'Why don't you get back to your birds?'

As I neared the haunted hill of Stapi I accelerated in case the gunman – Magnusson? – was lurking there. Then, as the playing-card roofs of habitation came into view, I slowed down and thought about Shirey.

What could I do to help him? Not much – except pursue my inquiries because I was sure it was all connected. Break the network and you would stifle the agitation. I could also go to the Café Trod and try and find some of the other guests at the party. I switched on the car radio and heard that demonstrations were being planned to demand Icelandic access to Shirey.

A group of long-haired students had gathered in one corner of the Trod coffee bar. Clean, not too matted, reading books on modern art over coffee long gone cold, occasionally glancing defiantly around in search of sneers.

Other young Icelanders were distributed around the place, not so shaggy, most of them wearing sweaters and flared trousers. In another corner sat an American sailor in uniform and another American in sportscoat, sharply-creased grey slacks and square black shoes. They looked puzzled and resentful, brooding over bottles of Coke.

The bar had modern furniture and lighting and some good painting around the walls.

The waitress brought me a jug of black coffee and a little jug of milk. I asked her if she remembered anyone answering Shirey's description in the café on Saturday. She said she did: he had looked so Scandinavian – more Scandinavian than Icelandic, she thought – and he had turned out to be American. He had been getting on very well with some young Icelandic people: this she liked to see.

I asked the waitress, who was dark and jolly and thirty-ish, if any of Shirey's acquaintances were in the café. She pointed at two boys of about eighteen, one in an Icelandic sweater, the other in a grey wool shirt. 'Those two,' she said. 'They were conversing wery vell.'

'Do the Americans get on well with the Icelanders here?'

'Usually they do.' Her jolliness wilted a bit. 'But the feeling is not so good now since that poor girl died. Those two American boys over there wanted to make friends with some Icelandic boys but it was no go.'

'Do you ever have trouble between Americans and Icelanders?'

She shook her head vehemently. 'Never the troubles. The

Icelandic young people are very keen to learn about America. The Americans want to know about Iceland. And they want to meet girls. Why should they not?' She sighed. 'If it was not for politics they would all be very happy together.'

'Wouldn't we all,' I said.

I joined the two Icelanders who had been with Shirey. They looked at me with hostility and finished their coffee. I asked them if they had been with a fair-haired, blue-eyed American on Saturday.

The boy in the wool-shirt said: 'Are you American?' He was thin and sensitive and prematurely assured.

'No. English.'

They relaxed a little. The same boy said: 'Why are you asking about some American, then?'

'He's in some sort of trouble and I want to help him. Did he go to a party with you that evening?'

'I do not know who you are talking about.'

'Do you remember him?' I turned to the other boy but his companion said: 'He doesn't speak English.'

'The waitress says you were with a fair-haired American on Saturday.'

'Then she is mistaken.'

'Why are you lying?'

'I am not.' He put some kronur on the table with the bill. 'What sort of trouble is this American in?'

'Very bad trouble. You could help him. I do not think he has done anything wrong.'

'You do not think assaulting and murdering an innocent girl is wrong?'

'I didn't mention the girl. Did you know her?'

He nodded hesitantly.

'Was she so innocent?'

'You do not understand the Icelandic mentality. If a girl and a boy are fond of each other then they sleep together.

This is not a loss of innocence: it is the most natural thing in the world. It is you people who make it seem dirty.'

'And what if a girl sleeps with many men?'

'It is her business.'

'You speak very good English.'

'My father was a diplomat in London for some time. I lived there for two years.' He melted slightly. 'I like it very much there.'

'Even with our dirty ways?'

'Different ways perhaps.' A slight strategic withdrawal. There was plenty of Icelandic patriotism in him; but he had already acquired a diplomatic defence mechanism from his upbringing.

'Why doesn't your friend speak English? Most young Icelanders do.'

'His father was a diplomat in Paris.' He smiled. 'Paris, France.'

We seemed to have established friendly relations. 'I promise you that this boy you met had nothing to do with the girl's death. Now, can you help me?'

But I had underestimated him. 'I do not believe you. He was seen with the girl.'

'The boy you were with in here?'

No such simple traps for Iceland's future representative in Washington, London or Moscow. 'No, the American boy you have just described.'

'You won't help?'

'Look.' He leaned forward to deliver his final speech. 'This is a dirty business. In Iceland we know nothing of murder or sexual assault. This crime could not have been committed by an Icelander. This American that you describe was seen with the girl at the Saga Hotel. He was also seen leaving with her. Shortly after that she was found dead. In those circumstances I cannot help you.' He stood up to leave.

'You mean she was found dead at about the time the American was arriving at the party?'

'What party?'

'So, you're falling for the Communist anti-American propaganda.'

'You don't even understand that. Communism in Iceland is not like Communism elsewhere. It is merely the voice of protest against the establishment. The true Opposition against the Government. Every democracy needs an opposition, does it not?'

I paid my bill and stood up. It was rather sad. 'I suppose you are a Communist?'

He nodded so defiantly that it was almost an apology.

'What would your father say?'

'He would understand.'

'I doubt it. He would know that even if your Icelandic Communism is different to doctrinaire Communism it is just as surely being used by the men in the Kremlin for their own purposes. Just as this poor girl's death is being used.'

'We are not so naïve as that.' He walked away with his friend and I felt almost sorry that I had implanted the doubt. But if he was going to be a diplomat he would have to learn.

Sleep was a long way off. I lay staring at a watercolour called *An Image from the Saga Period* by Asgrimur Jonsson and tried to dispel the image of Shirey's frightened face.

I considered ringing Gudrun then remembered that she was on a London flight.

I followed Shirey from the Saga Hotel through the light streets to the girl's home. The girl became a Russian with a scar above her crotch and heavy breasts.

'Don't worry,' my wife said. 'I burnt them as soon as I saw them. I guessed what had happened.'

But she turned away from me in the bed that first night and who could blame her?

'I'm sorry,' she said, months later. 'I'm so terribly sorry. I burnt the pictures but they're still with us. They always will be.'

'All right,' I said. 'But forget the pictures at the divorce. They mustn't be mentioned. I'll arrange everything.'

Shirey and I had both been fixed in much the same way. Was that the reason for my compassion for the pink-faced airman who didn't remotely comprehend the competing forces that had snared him?

I continued to stare at the helmeted warriors from the sagas until I joined them.

10

The Fugitive

The delegates to the conference on marine life were discussing sardines in a variety of languages and accents at the breakfast table while the landlady deplored the decline in morals that had resulted in the girl's death.

She presented each of us with a very hard-boiled egg. The Brazilian cracked his as if it were a skull, the Italian tapped his as if he expected an answer.

Rain sprayed the windows, a wind moved the branches of a birch tree in the garden. The landlady, who was grey and excessively maternal, was very proud of that tree.

She abandoned morals for weather. 'Soon the sun will shine and it will be vonderful,' she said.

The wonder of Iceland, I found, occasionally jarred. 'Do you know how many days it rained last year?' I asked.

She made a bird-like movement with her head. 'I do not know. But we have a beautiful climate here in the south because of the Gulf Stream. We have hardly any of the snow.'

'It's a simple statistic,' I said. 'It rained every day.'

The statistic stopped the sardine talk. 'It rain every day?' asked the Italian.

'Every day,' I said.

'*Mama mia*,' he said and dented his egg.

'In Iceland,' said the landlady, 'we have a saying about the weather.' She smiled at her cosmopolitan table, managing to exclude the cocksure English from her beneficence. 'We say, "If you do not like the weather, just wait a moment".' She replenished everyone's coffee cup except mine.

On the sideboard lay a copy of *Morgunbladid*. There was a picture of the dead girl as a schoolgirl on the front page. And underneath a police statement asserting that the girl, who was believed to have been in the company of an American serviceman that evening, had been under the influence of alcohol and may have died from asphyxia due to regurgitation. It added that no explanation had yet been found for a bruise on her mouth and the tearing of some of her clothes. Another news story said that civilian workers from the NATO base had reported that an American serviceman was being questioned by military police.

I picked up the newspaper and read the editorial. It was reasoned and reasonable. Homicide appeared to have been ruled out, but there were still a lot of unanswered questions. The torn clothing, the bruise, the alcohol content of the girl's blood. If the Americans were, in fact, holding one of their servicemen then they should at least give Icelandic police access to him in the interests of NATO relations. The editorial appealed for restraint, particularly among the younger sections of the populace.

I imagined what *Thjodviljinn* had to say about it and felt sorry for Charlie Martz.

There didn't seem to be a lot I could do for Fred Shirey.

So I asked the landlady for more coffee and thought about the job I had come to do. Somewhere, something didn't add up. My assailant hadn't been Hafstein because he had been at work. That left Laxdal or Magnusson of the known suspects – and instinct told me that it was Magnusson.

But why hadn't my attacker killed me? After all, they had tried the hard way once. It was as if they had been reassured rather than alarmed by finding me at Hafstein's house.

I sipped the coffee: it was cold. The talk at the Table of Babel had progressed to whitebait, so I left and returned to my room.

If my visit to Hafstein's home had given the general alarm to the Russian network then suspects like Magnusson would already be on the run. I went into the hallway and phoned Magnusson at his Reykjavik number. No reply. I tried his Westman Islands number and a woman answered. I asked to speak to Magnusson in what I hoped was immaculate Icelandic and waited for her to say that he wasn't at home. Instead she said: 'He is just finishing his breakfast – I will get him for you.' I hung up. Perhaps Sigurdson was wrong: he wasn't an agent.

I returned to my room to worry about it. Why was he still at home waiting to be taken in for questioning? He was hardly a hypnotised rabbit. And my presence at Hafstein's would surely have warned him that I was investigating key suspects. Unless he wasn't connected with Hafstein and presumed that I was suspicious only of the bearded lover of birds and churches. Perhaps he was working independently of Hafstein and Laxdal: a spy within a spy ring. Whatever the reason, Magnusson seemed to think he was sitting as pretty as a puffin on the cliffs of Heimaey.

I remembered Heimaey, the inhabited member of the Westman Islands, from my boyhood. A green valley encircled by razored cliffs, with men, intent on catching puffins, hanging from them on ropes like pendulums. The waves exploding all round and the smell of herring – the smell of money as they called it. The evocations called me. I decided to fly to Heimaey and interview Magnusson.

I consulted my Icelandair timetable. On the front was a picture of a blonde stewardess in her scarlet uniform:

Gudrun would be back from London this evening. There was a Fokker Friendship flight to Heimaey at 8.30 a.m. arriving at 8.55. I looked at my wristwatch: it was 8.59. If I went I would have to charter.

I switched on the radio and listened to the news on American Forces Network Iceland. It was mostly about a Wall Street recession with an interpretive piece by Walter Kronkite of CBS.

As I walked out of the room the phone in the hallway rang. I picked it up and Sigurdson's voice said: 'Conran?'

'Speaking. What's new, Einar?'

'Quite a bit,' he said. 'You'd better come down to my office.'

'Anything you can tell me on the phone?'

'Hafstein's vanished,' he said.

'Okay,' I said. 'I'll come down right away.'

At the front door the landlady was standing, arms akimbo as near as damn it. 'Look,' she said. 'The vonderful sunshine.'

'Yes,' I said, 'but just wait a moment.'

'How do you know he's skipped?'

'He didn't go back to his apartment in Reykjavik last night. He always gets to work at 8.30 in the morning. He hasn't turned up. Apparently he phoned the office twenty minutes ago saying that he wouldn't be in again for a while. He didn't say why.'

'Was it a local call?'

Sigurdson said it was.

'Then he's still in Iceland?'

Sigurdson nodded. 'I have alerted all ports and airports.' He poured us both coffee from the jug on his desk.

I said. 'The obvious place to go to is Hveragerdi.'

He looked at his gold watch. 'Okay, let's go.' He sounded like a television marine.

* * *

Three-quarters of an hour later Sigurdson braked his red Volvo sharply outside Hafstein's country residence. Steam blossomed around it and there was a man in dungarees in the hothouse. The front door of the house was ajar; Sigurdson looked cross as if he would have preferred to shoulder-charge it.

On the kitchen table was some half-eaten bread, cheese and *skyr* – the Icelandic version of yoghurt. Nothing in the lounge had been moved since my visit: it was a shop window in a neglected store – patina of dust on the TV, fruit crink-ling in a bowl on the sideboard. In the small bachelor bedroom there were signs of a hasty departure: the wardrobe door open, three freshly-laundered shirts lying across the bed, a grey wool sock on the floor, the bedside lamp knocked over.

Sigurdson said: 'The bird has flown.' It seemed singularly apt. He added: 'Whoever hit you must have warned him.'

'I don't think so,' I said.

In the study the birds were unruffled by it all. I checked the snowy owl – the bug was still there like an egg.

'Did your monitor pick anything up from this?' I asked Sigurdson.

'Nothing at all. Hafstein must have been by himself all the time.'

'What about phone calls?'

'Not one.'

Hafstein was either a master spy or an innocent at home. But if he was innocent why had he departed in such a frantic hurry?

Sigurdson said: 'We will have to pull this place apart,'

'I suppose so.' It didn't seem right somehow.

'I'll put a couple of the local police on to it and a finger-print man from Reykjavik.' He looked at me almost shyly. 'Dabs, I believe you call them.'

'Yes,' I said, 'dabs.'

I sat in Hafstein's chair behind the desk and stared out the gyrfalcon. Why, Hafstein? Why have you fled? Why have you forsaken your birds and your churches? What machinations of sophisticated intrigue have made you abandon all you hold dear?

And, incidentally, where the hell are you?

I opened the desk drawer. The paper on the migratory habits of the knot was missing. And so was the photograph of the girl who had sent her love to Hafstein long ago.

Sigurdson said: 'I'll bring in the man outside.' But the man outside was already inside, standing in the living room, not sure whether to be angry or frightened. He was about fifty-five, stringy, with a weathered face and large arthritic hands; there were snuff stains under his nostrils. He said in Icelandic: 'What are you doing in this house?'

Sigurdson showed him his identification and asked where Hafstein was.

The man shrugged and fingered his hairy nostrils. 'How should I know?'

Sigurdson stood in front of him, jacket tight around his chunky shoulders. He exuded menace without bothering with threats. 'When did you last see him?'

'Two days ago. He came to do some work in his study.'

'In the morning or evening?'

'In the evening.'

'Did you speak to him?'

'I spoke to him.'

'Where?'

The man pointed to the study with a crippled fore-finger. 'In there. We talked about the tomatoes. He has only just connected the steam from the hills and he is very concerned about them. I look after them. Watering and suchlike . . .'

His voice trailed away, withered by the disbelief on our faces. Two days ago I had installed the bug behind the snowy owl and it would have picked up the conversation between Hafstein and his handyman.

Sigurdson said: 'You're lying. Why?' He was very efficient at this sort of thing, less happy with the more sophisticated devices of detection.

The man produced a worn silver snuffbox from the pocket of his dungarees and took a pinch to win a little time. He sneezed, which was surprising from a seasoned snuff-taker; but then he wasn't concentrating on his vice.

Sigurdson opened his jacket and the man looked at the butt of the pistol stuck in the shoulder-holster. Sigurdson said: 'What is your name?'

The snuffbox slid back into the man's pocket. 'Thorarinsson,' he said. 'Eggert Thorarinsson.'

'When did you last see Hafstein?'

'I told you, two days ago.' He couldn't understand how we knew he was lying.

Sigurdson gave him a gentle push and he fell back into the cheap orange armchair. A cloud of dust arose from the new upholstery. 'We know you are lying. Now please tell us the truth. We don't want to get tough with you.'

'I can't remember.'

Sigurdson took off his jacket and put his gun on top of the TV set. You could see the outline of his vest under his shirt, and the muscle beneath the vest. He rolled one fist in the palm of the other. 'Start remembering,' he said.

'Please,' Thorarinsson said. 'I am a sick man.'

'When did you last see Hafstein?' Sigurdson moved nearer to Thorarinsson, his fist still clenched.

Thorarinsson examined the fist. 'This morning,' he said.

'How long ago?'

'About three hours ago.'

'Why didn't you tell us that before?'

'He asked me not to tell anyone.'

'Did he give you any money to encourage you to keep quiet?'

Thorarinsson hesitated.

'Did he?'

'He gave me my wages in advance because he said he would be away for some time.'

'How much?'

'I forget the exact amount.'

'Have you been home since Hafstein left?'

Thorarinsson shook his head.

'Then you still have the money on you.'

Thorarinsson nodded unhappily and took a pinch of snuff.

Sigurdson flicked his fingers. 'Come on, Thorarinsson, let's see how much he gave you.'

Thorarinsson took a wad of new notes and handed them to Sigurdson.

Sigurdson ruffled them with his thumb and said: 'You seem to be a very highly paid hothouse gardener.' He laughed for the first time that day. 'It is also a lot of money for a clerk in the Thjodskrain to be able to afford as a bribe.'

I said to Thorarinsson: 'Where did he say he was going?'

'He didn't say.'

'Come on,' I said. 'Where?' I asked, while Sigurdson menaced.

'He didn't say.' Thorarinsson was trembling, his eyes on the money in Sigurdson's hand. 'He didn't say. I swear it. He often went away without telling me where. In the summer he travelled all over Iceland looking at churches and birds. That was all he lived for. That and his tomatoes . . .'

He stopped speaking because Sigurdson had picked him up by the collar of his dungarees.

Thorarinsson yelped. 'I don't know where he went, Akureyri maybe. Or Hafnarfjödur. I don't know. I could tell you any place in Iceland just to stop you hitting me. But I am not a good liar.'

'That's true,' Sigurdson said. 'You're not.' He dropped Thorarinsson back on to the armchair which emitted dust again. He said to me: 'I think he's telling the truth this time. Hafstein could be anywhere in Iceland. Husavik, Grenivik, even Reykholt.'

'What's at Reykholt?' I asked.

'It was where Snorri Sturluson lived,' he said. 'A hot spring called Snorri's bath still exists there.'

'Of course,' I said. 'I'd quite forgotten.'

Thorarinsson stood up and asked if he could go.

'Tell us a bit about Hafstein,' I said. 'What did he do when he was here?'

Thorarinsson kept his eyes on the money. 'Kept himself to himself. He would either be in his study or in the hothouse. He was having two books published, you know. One about birds and one about churches.'

'Who was publishing them?'

'I don't know. Some firm in Sweden. I know he was very upset because he had to pay for the publication – no one would publish them otherwise. He had been working on the book about churches for about twenty years. He was very upset. He changed a lot after that.' His voice became conspiratorial. 'I think he was a little mad.'

Sigurdson shuffled the notes in his hand. 'In what way was he mad?'

'He talked a lot about the unfairness in the world. About the wrong values.'

'I thought you said he kept himself to himself,' I said. 'He seems to have been unusually talkative to an employee.'

'It was just one evening.' Thorarinsson smiled at Sigurdson because we were all collaborating so nicely. 'Can I have my money back now?'

Sigurdson's smile was equally friendly. 'No,' he said.

'Maybe when you've told us all you know,' I said. 'What did he say that one evening?'

'Nothing very much. We followed the pipeline into the hills because he thought the steam was losing power. It wasn't, in fact. He stood there looking down into the valley talking about all the worthless people who were getting away with dishonesty and deceit and how he would get his revenge. I didn't take much notice of what he said. He always paid me regularly and that was all that bothered me. But I think it turned him a little crazy when his book was rejected.'

'Anything else that evening?' I asked.

'Nothing much. He did say that he would make sure that he found the money to get his books published.'

Sigurdson leaned forward. 'By helping the Communists?'

Thorarinsson looked surprised. 'Not as far as I know.' He put out his lumpy hand. 'Can I have the money now?'

Sigurdson threw it at him and the notes scattered over his lap, over the floor. He knelt to pick them up.

I walked into the study and stared at the birds. You know the answer, I thought. Why don't you open your bloody beaks and squawk?

On the way back we made a diversion to the springs from which Hafstein was getting his steam. From one pipe, steam roared out forty feet or so in impotent fury. Elsewhere pools bubbled and steamed, and beside the path blisters of grey mud rose and popped like bubblegum. A stream ran down the hillside to the road where we had parked the Volvo: its bed was yellow with crystallised sulphur, a miniature yellow glacier.

On one side of the stream lay a pool of boiling hot mud with a board warning you not to get too close. The mud was grey and heaving. Now and again the heave of mud was stronger – like the theory of the seventh wave – and a small laborious fountain arose.

Above us stood the church. *Old, Roman Catholic, situate*

adjacent mud pools and hot springs, one km from Hveragerdi. Now disused.'

It was probably the sight of the church that had ignited Hafstein's anger that evening. Disused, deserted, treated with the same contempt that his books had been. But how was he going to exact his revenge?

Sigurdson was not particularly interested in disused Roman Catholic churches. Or any other churches. 'Let us get back to Reykjavik,' he said. 'I have alerted police all over Iceland to watch for Hafstein. There is little else we can do. Perhaps we will have a drink when we get back?' He looked at me hopefully.

'Perhaps,' I said.

'And after this is all over we must find some girls and have a party.'

'All right,' I said. 'After we've found some spies.'

I drove up to the base, and Sigurdson went to his office, stopping, perhaps, at the Hotel Borg bar on the way.

The military policeman and I were old buddies now. 'Just hold on, sir, while I call Commander Martz.' I thought I heard a groan on the other end of the phone.

'Jesus,' Martz said in his friendly way, 'you're all I need.'

'Are you interested in spies right now?'

'Nope. All I'm interested in right now is stopping about two thousand angry young Icelanders marching on this base. At the moment they're holding off until midnight because tomorrow is their National day and they'll have all the time in the world to wreck the joint.'

Charlie Martz, I thought, wasn't so different from Einar Sigurdson. The same heartiness that disconcertingly hardened into shrewdness when there was business to be done, the same chunky competence. Except that Martz was softer when it came to hurting the innocent; and was the better operator.

'Are you still holding on to Shirey?'

'Just about. The Ambassador's been on to the Admiral and the Admiral's been on to me. And do you know what I said? I said, "See here, Admiral, sir, Mr William Conran of British Intelligence has asked me to hold on to Airman First Class Shirey for just as long as I can because Mr William Conran believes he is innocent." And do you know what he said?'

'I can guess.'

'He said, "Tell Mr William Conran of British Intelligence to go fuck himself."'

'I'm not a contortionist,' I said mildly.

A glimpse of gold tooth. A small reward. The phone sounded and I wondered if he had ever checked to see if it was bugged. He did a lot of listening, then hung up.

'Trouble?' I asked unnecessarily.

Martz said that the demonstrators would start assembling at Reykjavik coach station at 10 p.m. They were coming by coach, bus, car, motorcycle. They would be at the main gate by midnight. By then the Icelandic police would have a formal charge ready to enable them to hold Shirey. If the Americans refused to hand him over there would be an official protest not to mention an invasion by the young people of Iceland. But, in fact, there would be neither protest nor invasion because by that time they would have handed Shirey over.

'And there's nothing I can do to stop it,' Martz said, 'unless you or Sigurdson can dig something up.' He added: 'In any case I'm not so darn sure that Sigurdson wants any developments that will stop Shirey being handed over. I reckon that guy wants to get rid of the Americans as much as the Russians.'

'Can I see Shirey again?'

'Sure, if you want. Why are you so concerned about this kid, anyway?'

'Because he's an innocent kid. And I don't want to see him used as cannon fodder for international politics.'

'Okay, okay.' He looked at me shrewdly. 'Like you were?'

'Maybe. Except that I wasn't an innocent kid.'

Martz nodded sagely. 'I guess not. But it seems to me that you're getting yourself a little too emotionally involved. However, that's your business. I don't want to see Shirey victimised.' He did a rapid patrol around his office. 'How is the spy-catching business? '

'Hafstein's skipped,' I said.

'Has he by Christ. When?'

I told him all about it.

'What are you going to do now?'

'I'm not sure. Work Magnusson over maybe.'

He picked up a flight report from his desk. 'There was another Soviet trawler in this morning. Same place again. So we've probably got another Russian wandering around some place.'

'I wonder they didn't try and stake a claim to Surtsey,' I said.

Martz grinned. 'They were too late. *Paris-Match* got there first and claimed it for the French.' He completed his office patrol. 'By the way, who's this guy Jefferey?'

'A shit,' I said.

'I figured that. He's been asking a few questions about you.'

'And did you answer them?'

'I told him to do what the Admiral thought yot1 should do,' Charlie Martz said.

I really did like Charlie Martz.

Shirey had been moved to a room in an unoccupied married quarter. It was furnished with a dressing table, a double bed and a wardrobe. A TV set had been installed and Shirey was reading the programmes in *The White Falcon*, the base's weekly paper. There were some comics on the bed, a *Playboy* and a skiing magazine. The tin ashtray was cluttered with cigarette butts.

'Hi,' I said.

He looked up from the paper and grunted. 'What's on television?'

He looked as if he wanted to say, 'What's it to you?' Instead he said: 'Nothing till four. Then it's the *Bob Cummings Show*.'

I gave him a cigarette. 'You must be pretty nervous.'

'Yeah.' No sirs now that Martz wasn't present: I was just another interfering foreigner. I didn't blame him.

'I met some of the Icelanders who invited you to that party.'

'Yeah? What did they say?'

'They said they didn't meet anyone answering your description in the Trod. The waitress told me they did meet you.'

'Lying bastards,' Shirey said. 'Just because I'm an American.' He stood up in front of the TV set, fair hair falling over his forehead, bright blue eyes shadowed. 'I'll tell you something, mister. I'm proud to be American. I wouldn't want it any other way. If it wasn't for us Americans the whole shitty world would be in the hands of the Communists by now. I wonder how they'd like it then – all these snide sons of bitches who want us out.' He paused and pointed a finger with a bitten nail in my direction. 'They're all jealous. That's what's wrong – all these stinking little countries are jealous.'

'No one likes being helped,' I said. 'They never have.'

He sat down in the chair again and went back to being scared. 'Anyway, what's in this for you?'

'I'm just trying to help. Something like this happened to me once.' I sounded like the visiting preacher at reform school.

'Yeah?' Interest flickered. 'Did you get caught screwing the Ambassador's wife or something?'

I remembered the Ambassador's wife. 'Nothing quite as unpleasant as that,' I said.

'What happened then?'

'I was framed with a Russian girl in Moscow. Photographed. You've probably read about that sort of thing.'

'Sure,' he said, 'I read about it.'

'It nearly cost me my career. It did cost me my wife.'

'Gee,' he said, 'I'm sorry.'

'So you see what I mean?'

'I don't see why it makes you want to help me.'

'I don't want to see the same sort of injustice happen twice. I was used just as you're being used now.'

'I guess so.' He began to shiver again, tensing his muscles to try and hide it. 'But what the hell can you do? I hear the Icelanders are marching on the base or something. They'll have to hand me over.'

'We can stall.'

'For how long? No one in their right mind is going to come forward and say they were responsible for the girl's death.'

'They might,' I said without conviction. 'It isn't rape or murder. The Icelandic people are pretty honest.'

'Yeah? Like those guys who invited me to the party?' He had given up trying to control the trembling. 'I appreciate your help, mister. But there ain't nothing you can do.'

There wasn't much more to say. Except, perhaps, to turn my collar round and tell him to have faith and not to give up hope. Even though there wasn't much hope.

'You didn't do anything to that girl, did you?'

He shook his head. 'Nothing more than I told you.' He looked much younger than his years at that moment.

'I'll see what I can do,' I said, even more inadequately.

I picked up *The White Falcon*. At 6 p.m. after Bob

Cummings and a couple of other shows, there was a show called *Wanted Dead or Alive*.

There was a message on my bed. 'Mr Sigurdson asked that you telephone him at once. It is very urgent.'

I phoned Sigurdson's office but he had left for the Westman Islands where a police officer had reported seeing Hafstein.

I drove to the city airport and chartered a small aircraft from a firm called Flugthjonustan. While they filled in the papers I called on Laxdal and told him to cancel our flight over Hekla; because I reckoned that if we got into trouble and there was only one parachute it wouldn't be strapped on my back.

'Where are you going now?' he asked.

I told him because he would find out anyway from flight control.

Twenty minutes later I was airborne, on my way to the Westman Islands, also known as The Grenadiers.

11

The Grenadiers

The Westman Islands lie seven miles south of the mainland of Iceland and one hundred miles by sea from Reykjavik. Fifteen tiny islands of tuff and basalt thrown up by volcanic action and nicknamed The Grenadiers by trawlermen because they resemble a line of guardsmen.

They are called the Westman Islands because Celts from the British Isles and Ireland were known by the Vikings – who first settled in Iceland as Westmen. And, according to the sagas, one of the Vikings, Hjorleifur, was murdered by his Irish slaves. The slaves were pursued by Hjorleifur's foster brother, Ingolfur Arnarson, and killed in the Westman Islands. That, anyway, was one theory for the name.

In the seventeenth century Algerian pirates raided Iceland returning home with a particularly good haul from the Westman Islands. They carried off 300 inhabitants and sold them as slaves in Africa.

If history, climate and geography has made the people of Iceland tough and intensely patriotic then this is doubly so of the people of the Westman Isles. In 1874, when Iceland was granted a constitution, bad weather prevented the

Westman Islanders from crossing to the mainland; so every year they celebrate their own National day during the first weekend in August, unlike everyone else in Iceland who celebrates it on June 17.

Today the 5,000 or so inhabitants regard themselves as a special community and talk half-jokingly about seeing autonomy in a world where there is currently no escape from separatism.

All the inhabitants live on Heimaey, a 4½ by 2 mile scrap of lava and grass kept verdant by the protecting masses of a precipitous crag called Heimaklettur and an extinct volcano called Helgafell. In the calm after the storms, of which there are many, these two guardians have an air of massive imperturbability which minimises human importance as effectively as an erupting volcano.

The local sport is puffin-catching and it says little for avian intelligence that the puffins continue to nest in the holes in the cliffs. They are caught by nets on poles as they fly towards their nests and are then cooked and eaten.

There are kittiwake, fulmar, guillemot and petrel to be seen. And many migrants bound to and from Western Europe. Which is why I should have remembered the mention of the Westman Isles in Hafstein's notes on the knot and realised that he might seek refuge here.

The islanders also make a sport of climbing the cliffs for eggs. And they make quite a show of it during their own national festival when a tented camp is struck and there is much merrymaking, dancing, feasting, drinking and coupling in the grass and on the lava which is very old and therefore not too sharp for that sort of thing.

The island's main exports are cod and herring and the little harbour jostles with fishing boats. In one year 8½ per cent of Iceland's total catch was landed there, and the smell of herring is strong in the saline air.

We flew low over the Icelandic mainland. Over mossy

lava, snow-veined mountains, lakes and geysers that looked like smoking cigarette ends from the aircraft. Primeval, aloof and yet beckoning on such a crystal day. Then the crinkled sea and The Grenadiers. And to the south the newest recruit to their ranks, Surtsey, which joined up in 1963 in a fountain of smoke and lava.

The pilot, fiftyish with many lines at the corners of his eyes, pointed at Surtsey. 'I flew around her when she first appeared. She was throwing out lava bombs which exploded when they hit the sea. And the red-hot lava was running down from the crater – 1,000 feet in fifteen seconds – and hissing and crackling in the water.' He looked over his shoulder. 'Do you want to take a quick look?'

There wasn't really time. 'All right,' I said. 'A quick look.'

It looked like a green and mauve whale. A whale on which life was beginning. As perhaps it had begun on earth. Moths, mussels, grass roots, seeds, seaweed.

On the lava beach a small boat had been landed; and half way between Heimaey and Surtsey another motor boat made an arrowhead in the water.

The pilot pointed down. 'Scientists,' he. said. 'They come from all over the world.'

'Okay,' I said. 'Now put down on Heimaey.'

A taxi took us from the airstrip to the small police station in Heimaey.

There was one policeman in the office. I asked him where Sigurdson was. He shrugged. 'I have no idea.'

'Are you the officer who spotted Hafstein?'

The policeman, who was broad and blue-chinned – the direct descendant of an Irish slave with an Algerian additive? – looked at me suspiciously. 'Who are you, if I may ask?'

I showed him my card; he was not particularly impressed. 'Sigurdson and I are working together.' If that impressed him it didn't show. 'Have you seen him?'

The policeman nodded: he was not a garrulous man.

'You've seen him but you don't know where he is?'

The policeman nodded.

'Are you stationed here?'

'Not usually. I come from the mainland.'

'Where did you spot Hafstein?'

The policeman pointed in the direction of the cliffs over-looking the harbour. 'He was climbing up there.'

'Climbing?'

'Yes, climbing. I am told Emil Hafstein was a very good climber. He was often here observing the birds. And often he would go to the Hotel Hamma and lecture the customers in the bar about puffin-catching. They listened because he bought them drinks.'

It was quite a speech for the policeman. I coaxed a little more from him. 'I suppose Sigurdson went up after him?'

The policeman picked up the authorisation papers that Sigurdson had given me and examined them more closely. Reluctantly he said: 'Yes. I informed Sigurdson in Reykjavik and he told me to keep watch on Hafstein while he flew over. Hafstein disappeared in a cave and I posted a man at the foot of the cliffs to keep watch on the cliffs. It was a perfectly good arrangement because it would take a man at least twenty minutes to reach the ground again from that cave – the cliffs are very steep just there.'

I guessed the reason for the policeman's reluctance to discuss the manhunt: he had botched it up. 'But when Sigurdson arrived Hafstein had gone?'

The policeman nodded and pulled on his white gloves as if to cover guilty hands. 'When Sigurdson arrived I drove him to the cliffs.' He examined a hole forming in one finger of a glove. 'We found the man – he was only a youth really – lying unconscious at the bottom of the cliffs.'

'How the hell had that happened?'

'I can only presume that Hafstein had dropped something on him.'

'He must have been a bloody good shot'

'That's what Sigurdson said.'

'Sigurdson was very angry?'

The policeman fingered his jaw as if Sigurdson had hit him. 'He was displeased.'

'And he climbed the cliff?'

'Yes – he is also a very good climber. But when he reached the cave he found that Hafstein had gone. I don't think it surprised him very much. But he must have found something up there because he immediately commandeered a motor boat and set out from the harbour.'

'But he must surely have told you where he was going?'

The policeman shook his head sadly and I felt almost sorry for him. 'He told me to mind my own business. He was very displeased.'

I pictured Sigurdson's displeasure and felt even more sorry for the stupid blue-chinned policeman whose true vocation was directing traffic. I sympathised, too, with Sigurdson.

I told the policeman to take me in his Volkswagen to the cliffs. He agreed and almost called me sir; an anti-social manner and a bristly chin can sometimes be very deceptive.

We stopped on the way at the Hotel Hamma so that the pilot could have a meal and I could have a drink. Because if I was going to climb the bloody cliffs with a rope tied round me I needed a brandy. Or two.

It was 1 p.m. The town, white and tin-roofed and fishy, was quiet. A few cars with youths and girls in them drove past, then reappeared, as they completed circuits of the place. The fishing boats, shouldered together on the quays, creaked and murmured on the slight swell. A man in his twenties staggered down the main street waving a Coca-Cola bottle, but the brown liquid inside must have been fortified because things seemed to be going better with Coke than the manufacturers had ever envisaged.

The bar in the hotel was closed. But a waitress gave me a brandy. In one corner a man drank vodka and ice dyed green with Crème de Menthe. In another a middle-aged woman drank thirstily at a whisky or brandy; her face looked vaguely familiar.

I phoned Reykjavik and asked if anyone there knew Sigurdson's destination – in case he had checked with them. No one knew.

'All right,' I said to the tamed policeman. 'To the cliffs.'

From the harbourside the sheer cliffs had the texture of baize. They were speckled with gulls – and puffins waiting to be netted, their orange-beaked clowns' faces wistful and fatalistic.

Ropes hung from the crags with children suspended from them.

'They are learning to climb for eggs,' the policeman said. 'Soon they will be as at home on the cliff-face as they are on the ground.'

We swung round the harbour passing two youths burning the feathers off a puffin with a blow-torch. They smiled pleasantly as we passed.

We stopped on the quayside and the policeman pointed at a rope idling against the cliff without a child weighting it. 'That was Hafstein's rope,' he said.

'Now it's mine,' I said without enthusiasm.

I had scaled cliffs in the Shetlands, on the Rock of Gibraltar, in the Urals, looking at birds and nests and eggs. But I had been fitter then, and younger; and in retrospect none seemed as steep as this. But if Hafstein could do it then so could I.

The policeman looked at me doubtfully. 'Perhaps I should go instead.' His voice cracked with hope that his offer would be declined.

'You would be no better than me.'

'Couldn't we send someone else up?'

'No,' I said. 'No one else.' I had issued the challenge to myself: I had to accept. People ridiculed us ornithologists: we had to prove ourselves.

I tied the rope around my waist and started to climb. Up the smooth foothills with ease, then up the first steep ascent using the rope the way they taught you in the commandos.

The green baize was cropped grass, moss and lichen. I moved lightly, exhilarated with my competence. I was half way up when I slipped. I fell a couple of feet, clenched at the rope burning through my hands, felt a razored rock slice at my calf. The rope stopped burning my hands: I had halted the fall. I swung idly for a moment, kicking at the cliff with my feet.

A small voice reached me from below. 'Are you all right?'

I didn't reply. I kicked out once more, found one foothold, then two. I rested and tried to think who would care if I killed myself. It didn't require much thought. I looked down at the harbour, which seemed as tranquil as artists always imagine harbours. And at the policeman staring up at me, wishing that he had never been posted temporarily to the Westman Islands, that Hafstein hadn't sought refuge here and that neither Sigurdson nor I had come in pursuit.

I looked to one side and found a puffin staring at me wondering why I hadn't caught him.

I climbed on, age asserting itself; heart galloping, breath rasping. Behind me I left a trail of blood: it looked very bright and ketchupy on the cushions of moss. But the leg with the sliced calf muscle was becoming weak. I kicked myself away from the cliff-face with my left leg and went on hauling. My biceps were getting weaker, too, and whenever I rested they twitched with a life of their own.

I gazed over the harbour, past its craggy guardians, over the metallic sea. Just me and the cliffs and the sea. A breeze played with the grass and above me somewhere I heard wings singing in the air. I hauled myself past a nest of baby puffins just hatched, growing up to be caught and eaten.

Then I was on the ledge from which the rope was suspended. Lying there sucking down air, waiting for the pain in my chest to fade. After a few minutes I sat up and examined my leg. My foot squelched in the blood that had collected in my shoe, and the blood was still trickling down my calf. I tore a strip off my shirt and bound it tightly above the wound. I looked regretfully at the tattered black leather of my Church's shoes.

Far below the policeman waved. I waved back. Then crawled into the black mouth of the cave.

After a few minutes my eyes adjusted themselves to the dusk inside. It was my closest contact with darkness since I arrived in Iceland. The only light came from the entrance and from a fissure in the roof.

Water dripped steadily somewhere in the interior. It was the only sound: the still air muffled all sound from outside.

But the air *had* been disturbed recently. On one side of the cave there were papers strewn all over the ground – the manuscript, perhaps, of a book that the author had dropped in his hurry to escape. And folders and a photograph catching some light on its gloss. On the other side of the cave there were tins of food, some books, a sleeping bag, an oil lamp and a box of matches.

Emil Hafstein had anticipated flight and pursuit. I wondered how he had hoped to keep the islanders away from his refuge.

I lit the lamp with the matches. My blood looked very dark in the oily light. But the bleeding had stopped.

I shuffled through the papers. It was a carbon copy of his book on churches. Beside it was the paper on the migratory habits of the knot containing the references to the Westman Islands. Heimaey was obviously Hafstein's second sanctuary. Here he found peace – and plotted vengeance. But against whom?

Hafstein's heaven, I thought, would be a lonely atoll of primeval grandeur feathered with birds and crowned with an ancient church.

I crawled around the cave looking for the clue which Sigurdson had found to Hafstein's next refuge. But all I found was the skeleton of a puffin and the source of the iced water dripping from the roof.

I lit a cigarette and blew the smoke over the top of the wavering flame. Lastly I picked up the photograph of the girl who had once sent her love to Hafstein. Then I knew why the face of the woman in the Hamma Hotel had been familiar.

'You should go to the hospital to have that leg seen to,' the policeman said. Heimaey had a hospital as well as a cinema, a dance hall, a bank and a telephone exchange.

'Just get me back to the hotel,' I said.

'Very well.' The beetle Volkswagen jerked forward round the harbour.

'Hafstein had prepared himself for a siege up there,' I said.

'So Mr Sigurdson said.'

'How the hell was he going to keep all your egg-climbers away from the cave?'

'They wouldn't have gone near it.'

'Why on earth not?'

'Because it is said to be haunted.' He smiled apologetically as Icelanders do when they mention the supernatural. 'I expect Hafstein spread the story himself.'

The woman was still in the corner with a drink in front of her. And the man was still contemplating his green vodka with understandable suspicion.

I sat down in front of the woman and said: 'Where's Hafstein?'

The drink was whisky and she had drunk more than one. She was middle-aged and had given up caring about her appearance long ago. A shawl hung round her shoulders, her greying hair was dull, her features still retained character but the flesh covering them had lost interest.

She looked up slowly from her drink. 'Who are you?'

'It doesn't matter. Where's Hafstein?'

'He's gone,' she said. As if for ever.

'It is important that I find him.' I ordered a brandy and a large whisky from the hovering waitress. 'Important for Iceland.'

'What do I care about Iceland?' She peered at me muzzily. 'What do you care about Iceland?' She poured the old whisky into the new and drank thirstily.

'You were once very fond of Emil Hafstein. A long time ago.'

'*Djofullin sjalfur!* A long, long time ago. So long ago that it doesn't matter. We have both lived another lifetime since then.'

'You are married?'

'I am a widow.' She peered at me through the haze of alcohol. 'What does it matter to you?'

'I want to help.'

'No one can help. Not now.'

'Did you hit the man who was guarding the foot of the cliffs with a rock?'

She nodded. 'I just stood there talking to him. He didn't suspect a woman. Why should he? Then I pointed at the cave. When he looked up I hit him with a stone.'

'You could go to prison for that.'

'What do I care?'

'Please help,' I said. 'I want to help Hafstein.'

'Help? You will only betray him. The way everyone has.' She finished the whisky and pushed the empty glass towards me. 'The way I did.'

'Because you married someone else?'

She nodded heavily. 'Then I watched him grow old and felt myself grow old as I bore my husband's children. Now it is too late, everything is too late.'

I wondered why she had married someone else. A lover's quarrel, parental pressure. Perhaps Hafstein had doubted his capabilities as a lover. Perhaps . . . 'You could still be happy together,' I lied.

'Not now. Emil is a little mad. I am old and no longer attractive. There is nothing left for us.'

'But you still loved him enough to warn him that the police were coming over from the mainland.'

'News travels fast in Heimaey. Yes, I warned him. He heard me calling him from the bottom of the cliffs. I think he was watching all the time.'

'And then he fled by boat?'

'There is no other way to flee from Heimaey unless you can fly an aeroplane.'

I leaned forward, staring at the mottled hand, searching for the real truth. 'What was he fleeing from? What was he frightened of?'

'I don't know,' she said. 'He never told me.'

'But he used to come here often?'

'Yes, but not to see me. It was just a coincidence that I lived here.'

'And he never told you what he was frightened of?'

'Never.' She was telling the truth.

'Did he never tell you why he left all those provisions in the cave?'

'Just as a place to escape. From everyone. As I say, he was a little mad. He said everyone's values were wrong. He was upset that no one really wanted to publish his books. Sometimes he talked about revenge. I didn't ask him what he meant. I just listened and pretended that it was all happening many years ago.'

She started to cry.

'Did he suddenly seem to have a lot of money?'

She nodded; the tears splashed on the table and into her whisky. I ordered another and refused myself another brandy. The man in the corner plucked up courage, downed his green drink and left.

'Are you sure you don't know where he's gone?'

'I didn't say I didn't know.'

'Where has he gone then?'

'He has gone to die.'

'To commit suicide?'

'He has gone to die. To a place where he will be alone. To be as close to the earth and as far away from the values that he hated as it is possible to be.'

To the atoll with the church and the friendly birds. The boat on the beach, the boat in pursuit . . .

'Where is that?' I asked. But I knew already.

'To die where life is beginning.'

'He's gone to Surtsey?'

She nodded. I should have known; just as I should have known about the Westman Islands. Once upon a time I would have been quicker.

I bought her another whisky. Then I went down to the harbour and hired the fastest motor boat I could find.

12

The Fire-Bringing Giant

You could see Surtsey, named after Surtur the fire-bringing giant from Norse myths, quite plainly from Heimaey. A basking whale, black against the bright sky.

It first made its presence known when fishermen saw a glow under the waves and found that the water was hot. Within a week Surtsey had grown to a height of forty metres and a length of 500 metres. In April 1964 it entered into what they called its Strombolian phase, hurling lava bombs 300 metres into the air. And the red lava streams that doused themselves in the sea strengthened the new island's foundations so that it didn't slip away again like so many recruits who just faded away since The Grenadiers paraded permanently in the ninth century.

The eruption continued in 1966 then settled with an area of about three square miles.

The Westman Islanders claimed it for themselves. So did *Paris-Match*. But Surtsey belonged to Iceland and the scientists of the world, and that is how it stayed. A mauve and green island of lava, changing shape, forming its own ashy beaches, permitting the electrolysis of life to start as perhaps it had started on earth at the beginning of time.

The scientists had kept it as sterile as possible and they would not welcome Emil Hafstein or his pursuers as they had welcomed the first moth or the first flower, which had been the Sea Rocket.

The motor boat was very fast and we raced past the minute islands of Sudurey, Hellisey and Sulnasker.

The fisherman at the wheel slowed down as Surtsey swam up in front of us, about two miles away.

'You want to take some photographs?' he asked.

'Just keep going,' I said.

Waves were slapping the bows now and a dark cloud had appeared in the sky as Surtsey had once appeared in the sea.

The fisherman, about eighteen, young, pale and hard, said: 'Soon it will storm.'

'Too bad,' I said.

He gave his Icelandic friendliness another try. 'Do you know what they say about the weather in Iceland?'

'Just wait a moment . . .'

'You know.' He swung the boat so that a wave sprayed over me.

We ploughed on as the clouds gathered. The waves chopped harder and the spray reached both of us. Soon it mixed with rain. My jacket and flannels stuck to my body, the dried blood was swabbed from my leg. My hair was plastered over my forehead Hitler fashion. The helmsman smiled at me with satisfaction.

Behind us Heimaey disappeared in the rain. And a couple of other Grenadiers with it. We were about a mile from Surtsey which in the stormy light looked as if it were made of blended plasticines, the way children mix them.

I saw the boat grounded on the tiny beach, and another one nearby. The wind blew straight at us, helping Surtsey to repel invaders.

At the base of the plasticine cliff I saw a cough of light. Then we heard a crack.

The fisherman looked puzzled. 'Thunder?' He shook his head; it was nothing like thunder. 'Did you hear that?'

I nodded into the rain and spray. 'I heard it.' Water filled my mouth and the wind snatched my words.

'Perhaps it was Surtsey starting up again?'

I shook my head violently so that he wouldn't be deterred by the fact that someone had just fired a gun on the world's newest island.

As the boat approached the last run of waves on to the beach I saw Sigurdson crouched behind a crag of lava, gun in hand. To his right, about seventy-five yards away, Hafstein leaned against another crag; he also had a gun. It was the first time I had seen Hafstein in person.

I shouted to them but the words flew out to sea. I knew what was going to happen; knew I would witness it; knew I could do nothing about it.

The fisherman shouted at me. 'What is going on?' He slowed down the motor. I grabbed the wheel from him and we accelerated.

'Hey!' shouted the fisherman.

'Shut up,' I said.

Sigurdson turned and recognised me. He put up one hand. *Stop, stay away, leave it to me.* If I could steer the boat in behind Hafstein there might be a chance of taking him alive. But it was too late. The waves were breaking on the shore, carrying us with them, breaking over the stern of the boat in clouds of spray.

Then Hafstein spotted us. He levelled his pistol. Above the roar of the waves I heard the shot. God knows where the bullet went; not in the boat, not in the fisherman or me. I felt for the Smith & Wesson cold against my sopping shirt.

As the boat ground on to the shore I heard another shot. Nearer – from Sigurdson. And Hafstein was falling, gun pointing at his own feet, one hand pawing at his chest.

But there were *three* people on the beach. As Hafstein fell the third, in yellow oilskins and sou'wester, ran out from behind Hafstein. Sigurdson raised his gun, then lowered it again.

I ran through the spent waves, but the figure in yellow reached Hafstein first. Hafstein was lying on the mauve and black cinders, blood flowing from the wound in his chest. He was dead. Sigurdson joined us.

The man in yellow stood up and said: 'Who are you?' His thin intelligent face, streaming with water, was contorted with fury.

Sigurdson said: 'More to the point, who are you?'

'I am a scientist studying the birth of life. Now, who are you?' He pointed at Hafstein. 'This man I know – but who are you and why did you kill him?'

The strength of the rain was diminishing and the sky on the horizon was bright blue.

Sigurdson put away his gun. 'I killed him because he was trying to kill me.' He handed the scientist his police pass covered in transparent plastic. 'What were you doing here?'

The scientist's fury was waning, to be replaced by an irradicable sadness. 'I was staying in the hut. We have a hut here, you know . . .' His voice meandered on incoherently.

The sun came out and the wet ash began to steam.

Hafstein's eyes were still open and his little beard stuck out determinedly above his loose neck. The gun still in his hand looked incongruous.

'How did you know this man?' I asked the scientist who had sucked-in cheeks, tufty eyebrows and passionate eyes.

'He used to come here. He had special permission because of his interest in birds.'

'The knot?'

'And others.'

Sigurdson said: 'I shall want you as a witness.' He turned to me. 'You, too, perhaps. And that fellow.' He pointed at the fisherman who had just succeeded in pulling the boat clear of the waves. 'We will take the body back to Heimaey.' He knelt and went through Hafstein's pockets. 'It is a pity. Now perhaps we shall never know . . .'

The scientist said: 'It is ruined now.'

'What's ruined?' Sigurdson asked.

'Our concept.'

'What concept?'

'To keep this island free of contamination.'

'This won't make any difference,' Sigurdson said.

'It is not just a question of physical contamination.'

Sigurdson grunted and called to the fisherman to help him move the body. 'It is a pity,' he repeated. 'A great pity. He was our man – I am sure of that.'

'I'm not so sure,' I said.

The scientist said: 'Now already Surtsey has been contaminated by human behaviour.' He took off his sou'wester revealing thin sandy hair. 'Surtsey was the beginning of time, the answer to everything . . .'

Sigurdson, who had never displayed leanings towards metaphysics, looked at me and shrugged, indicating impatience with all eccentricity.

We put Hafstein's body in the boat that had brought Sigurdson to Surtsey. Sigurdson took the scientist's name and address; we prepared to leave.

I put a last question to the scientist. 'You reached Hafstein first. Did he say anything?'

The scientist looked at me vaguely. 'Only two words.'

Sigurdson said: 'What were they?' His voice sounded angry from having to ask.

'He said, "German church".'

What the hell did that mean? Nearly all the churches in Iceland were German in a sense because of their Lutheran origins.

Sigurdson said: 'Is that all?' His tone implied that the scientist should have extracted more from the dying man.

'That was all.'

'It doesn't mean anything,' Sigurdson said accusingly.

'It must mean something,' I said. 'I think it probably means a lot.'

Sigurdson said: 'We must pull in Magnusson and Laxdal now – if they're still around.' We crunched down the cinders to the two boats. 'Shall we accompany Hafstein back to Heimaey?'

'If you wish,' I said. I told the fisherman I would meet him at the harbour and pay him.

The sky was still clear, the sea much calmer. I waved to the scientist but he took no notice. We joined the corpse in the boat and headed for Heimaey.

I looked back at Surtsey once more, when we were a few hundred yards away. The scientist was kneeling on the cinders, a bright yellow figure on the burnt virgin island. He was probably looking at the blood losing itself in the ash: the last evidence of death on the island where he had gone to observe the birth of life.

'The Garden of Eden,' I said.

'It doesn't look much like the Garden of Eden,' Sigurdson said.

'I was speaking figuratively.'

'Ah,' he said.

We flew back in my aircraft. Magnusson had flown to the mainland and Sigurdson had converted his disappointment into anger at the blue-chinned policeman.

The little aircraft bucketed around in high winds.

Sigurdson explained that the blue calm had merely been the centre of the storm.

We bounced along the runway at Reykjavik and the wind tried to tug us on to the grass.

As we climbed out I said: 'By the way, what did you find in the cave that led you to Surtsey?'

He looked rather proud of himself. 'There was a picture of Surtsey lying just at the mouth of the cave. He had written on top of it *The Final Refuge*. He must have dropped it in his hurry. He had been scribbling on it. What do you call that scribbling?'

'Doodling,' I said.

'Yes, doodling. He had drawn a lot of birds on the rocks and a little church on the top.'

13

The Latchkey belonging
to a Girl working in
the office of a Barrister

Charlie Martz told me on the phone that diplomatic pressure
to force the Americans to hand Shirey over was building
up.

'Have they named Shirey yet?'

'Not yet. Have you dug up anything that could justify us
holding on to him?'

'I'll tell you later,' I said – because I hadn't dug anything
up. 'I'll be coming up your way.'

'I guessed you would,' he said. 'There's a flight due in
from London, isn't there?'

'All in the line of duty,' I said.

'Sure,' he said. 'But what do I tell this creep Jefferey?'

'The same message,' I said.

'Okay – but he must be getting quite sore by now because
I keep giving him the same message.'

I didn't ask whether he meant physically or mentally
sore. The other development during the visit to the Westman

Islands was that Laxdal was missing. He had taken off an hour before we returned. I checked with traffic control but he hadn't given a destination.

I let myself into his office. He had left behind a strong odour of aftershave. I opened the drawer of his desk: the picture of Gudrun had disappeared. I checked the phone: the bug was still there.

I didn't think we had lost him. He hadn't found the bug and like Magnusson he thought that my inquiries were centred on Hafstein. Now that Hafstein was dead the crucial time for Laxdal and Magnusson would be the next twenty-four hours: during that time they would discover whether my only prey had been Hafstein.

Despite Sigurdson's suggestion I decided against an immediate confrontation with either of them. The next few hours would be just as crucial for us. If they were happy that I had been concentrating only on Hafstein then it proved that Hafstein was unconnected with the infiltration of Russian agents.

But why had Gislason, the agent whom the Icelandic policeman had shot in the forest, kept Hafstein's name in his pocket? It was, among other things, amateurish. Granted, Soviet espionage was frequently amateurish – as were the espionage organisations of most countries – but that was sheer blundering.

The only protagonist with whom I had not yet made any sort of contact was Magnusson.

I let myself out of Laxdal's office and walked across the grass to the coach station. It reminded me of Russia. Spacious and modern and soulless, with a girl with a transparent blouse and black brassière selling tickets inside a glass cage. The girl in the apartment in Moscow had worn a black brassière.

I ordered coffee at the bleak 'Russian' bar. The whole building had been designed as if Iceland were an offshore island of the Soviet Union. Only the massive docility – a docility founded on fear – of the waiting passengers was missing. It was my job to ensure that such docility was never forced upon the Icelandic people. I had to find out about Magnusson, the enigma in the cast.

I phoned Sigurdson and said: 'Did you make that fitting in the trawler owner's office?'

'We did,' Sigurdson said. So Magnusson's office was bugged, too.

'Any results?'

'Nothing of importance. Mostly talk about cod and herring.' He rejected reticence on the phone as unnecessary. He said: 'By the way, that bullet was British.'

'I wouldn't have wanted it any other way,' I said. 'And I'd like to hear the tapes from Magnusson's office some time.'

'Now?'

'No, not now. Tomorrow, perhaps.'

'Of course,' he said. 'The Icelandair flight is due in from London.'

Were we all watching each other? And wouldn't it have been much easier if we had employed some agency to do the job?

'All in the line of duty,' I said.

'When should we question our two friends?'

'Not yet,' I said. 'I'm not convinced it's the right thing to do.'

'I've had all the papers from the cave picked up. If you want to study them they are at your disposal.'

'Later,' I said.

He laughed. 'Don't forget that we will find some real girls when this is over.'

'I won't forget,' I said. But there didn't seem to be much wrong with the one I'd got.

As I left the phone kiosk a small girl pointed me out to her mother. I remembered that my drip-dry clothes hadn't dripped completely dry and that my trouser leg was stained with blood.

I took a taxi back to the city airport and waited while the driver compared the conversion chart with the price on the meter – the meters couldn't keep up with devaluation in Iceland. The cab drivers in Reykjavik seemed to be more honest than most; Muscovite cab drivers had also been comparatively honest. I drove back to Baragata, changed, then pointed the Chevrolet towards Keflavik and felt excited because I was meeting my girl. At the same time I wondered if she would have considered it immoral to have slept with the pilot in one of the hotels adjoining London Airport – bearing in mind her relationship with me.

Once again I accelerated past Stapi. Who had taken a shot at me there? Magnusson, probably. Certainly not Hafstein. And sniping was somehow out of character with Laxdal: he was too flamboyant as if he were trying to cover up a defect in his personality – cowardice perhaps.

German Church. What German Church? Hafstein had been interested in every bloody church in Iceland. The only church I could directly connect him with was the church beside the mud pools. But that was Roman Catholic, possibly the least German church on the island.

I went first to the base and found Charlie Martz in his quarters with his wife and two daughters. His wife was a good-looking, hospitable woman in her thirties, happy to be wherever her husband was but wishing he were some- where else; his daughters were pretty and bouncy and wore white knee-socks. *Route 66* was on the television; they switched it off.

Martz poured us both some whisky in chunky glasses crammed with ice. The girls, aged about eleven and twelve, sat cross-legged on the floor and stared at me with interest that didn't flatter.

'I hear you're an ornithologist,' Mrs Martz said.

I said I was. She addressed the girls. 'Why don't you two do something like that?'

'What is it?' one of them asked.

'Bird watching,' Mrs Martz said.

'Oh,' they said, and disappeared into their bedrooms.

Mrs Martz persevered. 'I believe you're studying the fall-out from Hekla.' She must have guessed that I had other interests.

'That's right,' I said. 'I hear you're having a show of a rather different kind here tomorrow.'

'You mean the demonstration? It's all such a pity. Relationships were getting so much better.'

'It's a pity the servicemen aren't allowed to stay in town in the evenings,' I said. I turned to Martz. 'Incidentally Charlie, why aren't they? They're not vampires . . .'

'We just like to play it safe,' Martz said. 'We don't want to give the Commies any ammunition. It only needs one fight over a girl and you've got trouble. You know how it is – girls in any part of the world like a change. The Icelanders are tough, brusque, rough guys. It only needs some smooth-talking jerk from Los Angeles or Chicago or some place to move in on one of their girls and wham! – you've got yourself a brawl.'

'So 3,000 Americans have to be off the streets because you're afraid a handful of Communists might make capital out of a good healthy punch-up?'

Martz drank deeply and the ice clicked against his teeth. 'I didn't make the rules. And I didn't say I agreed with them.'

Mrs Martz said: 'Would you like another drink, Mr Conran?'

I gave her my glass. My leg was hurting and I felt bad-tempered. 'Do you like it in Iceland, Mrs Martz?'

'I like to be where my husband is.' She qualified this.

'It's not too bad in the summer. It's just like being in a small American town out here. But I don't look forward to the winter, Mr Conran. A couple of years back a little girl wandered off one evening. She wasn't gone long. But when they found her she had fallen in a snowdrift and was almost frozen to death. We have something here in the winter called the Chill Factor.'

'l know,' I said. 'Charlie told me about it.'

I looked around the room and envied them their comfortable domesticity on a lava field. Even with the Chill Factor. Tall paper flowers in the corner, mementoes from Charlie's ports of call, photographs of the kids as babies, lived-in furniture.

Martz had probably told his wife about my private life because she remained gracious despite my bad temper. 'I like the Icelandic people,' she said.

I grinned. 'You should – they discovered America after all.' I took a drink of Scotch dodging the rocks. 'In fact you could argue that the Icelanders are responsible for bringing the Americans here.'

She looked puzzled. 'I thought Christopher Columbus found America.'

'Leif Ericsson got there first. He was the son of the explorer Eric the Red and he was born in Iceland. He reached the American coast in A.D. 999 – centuries before Christopher Columbus.'

Mrs Martz looked inquiringly at her husband. Martz said: 'Billy boy's right for once. Ericsson called it Vinland. In 1965 they found a map of Vinlanda made in the fifteenth century. It was unveiled at Yale – on Columbus Day. The Spaniards and Italians in the States defended Christopher like crazy and a slogan appeared on a wall in Boston – "Leif Ericsson is a Fink".'

'Well I never,' said Mrs Martz.

Martz said to his wife: 'I wonder if you would excuse us

for a few moments. We're helping Bill with some of his research and the conversation is liable to get a little technical.'

'Why, of course,' she said, having heard similar requests many times before. 'I'll go and tell the kids all about that Fink Ericsson.'

'Well?' Martz said when she had gone.

I told him about Hafstein's death.

'Jesus Christ,' he said. 'Did Sigurdson have to shoot to kill?'

'He didn't have much option, Charlie. Hafstein fired first.'

'So that's our principal lead dead and gone.'

'I don't think he was our principal lead.'

'Then what the hell did he take off like that for? What was he doing bribing hothouse attendants and what was he doing with all that dough? What's more, what was he doing making himself a hidey-hole up there with the puffins?'

'I don't know,' I said. 'It's just a hunch. Magnusson and Laxdal didn't seem to give a damn as long as we were after Hafstein. That doesn't figure, does it, Charlie?'

He grunted and rubbed his scalp as if he were massaging his brains. 'Perhaps they knew that Hafstein wouldn't incriminate them.'

'You just said he was our most important lead.'

He sloshed some more Scotch into my glass. 'Maybe we should give Magnusson and Laxdal a going over. We're getting nowhere very fast at the moment.'

'We've got nothing on them,' I said. 'Communism's no crime in this country. And Magnusson is quite an influential man. Rough him up and you'll really be in trouble.' I paused. 'In any case I think they're more valuable to us the way they are.'

'So what do we do, wise guy?'

'There you have me,' I said. 'But we must keep tabs on

them. I will try and get closer to Magnusson. And we can go through the records that Hafstein was in charge of with a fine-tooth comb. And we can try and figure out what Hafstein meant by *German church*.'

'You'll have to figure it out pretty darn quickly,' Martz said.

'The records might produce a clue. That's why the agent the policeman shot had Hafstein's name in his pocket. Somewhere there's a list of all the agents and sympathisers in Iceland. We might get on to something tomorrow.'

Martz sighed, finished his Scotch and went to the window. On the cindery grass outside some boys were playing primitive baseball. He said: 'Forget Magnusson and Laxdal for a moment. I've got bad news for you.'

'You're handing Shirey over?'

'Right. At midnight tonight. There's no use kicking up a fuss. It's all fixed. We can't risk trouble on their National day.'

'But you said . . .'

'I know what I said, Bill old buddy. I only just got the call. The deadline for Shirey's release is midnight and that's all there is to it.'

The plane was late. I hung around in the lounge for fifteen minutes examining the souvenirs; paintings, carvings, lava ornaments, woollens, all expensive.

I read the newspapers which were full of reports about the demand to the Americans for access to Shirey, so far unnamed, and the celebrations planned for tomorrow.

I reached over the counter to examine the postcards of Surtsey and Hekla and the Great Geyser which, as long ago as 1907, had needed a dose of soap to make it spout for the King of Denmark. At the same time a corpulent man standing beside me also reached across and shouldered me to one side.

Instead of apologising he stayed in the same position flicking through *Iceland in a Nutshell* with thumb and forefinger. My leg was still hurting and I turned casually, catching him in the belly with my elbow; the belly was surprisingly hard.

We both turned and looked at each other. At last I had made contact with Olav Magnusson.

Instinct and training reacted. To show recognition was tantamount to confessing suspicion. I maintained icy English displeasure. 'Excuse me,' I said, and grabbed at some postcards, still gouging his stomach with my elbow.

He stood back. 'I am very sorry.' Good English, slight American accent.

'That's all right,' I said, treading firmly on his foot.

'Mr William Conran, is it not?'

Now what, I thought, is your game? 'Yes,' I said, in the voice English people use for discouraging vendors of pornography.

'I thought so. I have seen your photograph.'

'I doubt it very much.'

'But I assure you I have. You have come to Iceland to help us treat the sheep and cattle poisoned by Hekla, have you not?'

'That's true,' I said guardedly.

'I have read all about you.' He produced a folded newspaper from the inside pocket of his expensive, charcoal-grey suit. 'Look.'

I looked at myself leering stupidly from an inside page. Where the hell had the picture come from? From Whitehall, I presumed, to authenticate my cover. And inserted by whom? Jefferey, probably, with a sneer and a giggle as he remembered other photographs of me.

'That's certainly me,' I said.

'Are you waiting for the London plane?'

'I am as it happens.'

'Look,' he said. 'I have just dropped by to buy some periodicals because I happened to be in Keflavik. But I am extremely interested in the problems arising from the eruption and I should be most honoured if you would have a coffee or a drink perhaps with me.'

'The plane will be here any minute,' I said. 'So if you don't mind . . .'

'Please, Mr Conran. Be my guest. We get very hurt in Iceland if our hospitality is rejected.'

I gave him my aristocratic *damn foreigners* look. Why was he chancing his luck? On the other hand it didn't really matter to him whether we talked or not. And the conversation might indicate whether or not I suspected him. 'Very well,' I said. 'It's very kind of you.' *If you must*, my tone implied.

We had the usual jugs of coffee and milk and examined each other. He was as I had imagined him from the photograph and description supplied by Sigurdson. Muscle relaxing into fat, cheeks tinged with the pink sheen of good living, greying pomaded hair, clothes made in London, hair snipped inside his ears and tweezered out of his nostrils.

If he were a Communist then he modelled himself on the elite of the Kremlin, those with the town apartments, the country dachas and the big black Chaika limousines.

The mutual examination continued interrupted by coffee-table pleasantries. I knew him: he knew me: neither could reveal our knowledge. We both had to be very careful.

He stirred his coffee and said: 'I understand that the amount of lava from Hekla has surpassed already the amount of lava from the Askja eruption in 1961.'

'It surpassed it almost a month ago,' I said. I didn't think Olav Magnusson knew too much about volcanic fall-outs.

He sensed that I had the advantage and feinted from another direction. 'I have always had a very soft spot for the British.'

A total lie. And one calculated to make me react immediately because, if I had been studying him, then I would
have known about his part in the Cod War. He watched
me closely through the steam from his coffee.

'I'm very glad to hear it. I, too, am very fond of the
Icelandic people.'

'Really. You have been here before, Mr Conran?'

'I was born here,' I said. 'It's all in that newspaper report.'

'Ah, so it is.' He popped a sweetening tablet into his
second cup of coffee. 'So you have travelled all over our
country?'

'Not all over it.'

'Have you perhaps been to the Westman Islands?'

Again the tricky question. If my only concern were volcanoes there would be no point in denying my visit. Obviously
he knew that I had been there. 'It's funny you should say
that,' I said. 'I've only just returned. I'm something of an
ornithologist as that newspaper report says.'

'Ah yes, we have some wonderful birds there.'

'We?' Full marks, Conran.

'Yes, I forgot to tell you – I have a house on the Westman
Islands. Did you have any luck? Bird watching that is?'

'I saw plenty of puffins.'

He stroked his polished jowls. 'But they surely are of no
interest to an experienced ornithologist such as yourself?'

At least he couldn't fault me where birds were concerned.
'I was, of course, more interested in migratory species.'

'Ah yes,' he said. 'And how long do you propose to stay
in Iceland, Mr Conran?'

Outside I saw the serpent face of a 727 nosing across the
tarmac.

'About a month,' I said. 'Maybe longer. I want to help
you people solve this problem once and for all.'

'If I can be of any assistance at all, Mr Conran, please
don't hesitate to get in touch.' He produced a thin

crocodile-skin wallet and gave me a card made of wafer-thin wood – the sort they made in Hong Kong.

'That's very good of you Mr Magnusson.' I read his name aloud from the card.

'You are meeting a friend off the London plane?'

'An acquaintance.'

'Ah.' He lit a small thin cigar. 'A lady?'

'A lady.'

He made one last attempt to see if I knew anything about him. 'You must come and visit me on my farm. You might be able to study the effects of the fall-out on my animals at your leisure.'

'That's very kind of you. What do you have – sheep or cattle?'

The wariness relaxed a little. 'Very little animals, Mr Conran. But very valuable. I own a mink farm. At the moment all my mink come from Scandinavia. But soon I hope to breed Icelandic mink. They have been regarded here as vermin for too long. Soon I will have Icelandic mink that will be on show in the best salons of Paris and London. Do you know,' he added irrelevantly, 'that it took 5,000 skins to find the seventy to make a coat for Gina Lollobrigida?'

I said I didn't know. Passengers were pouring out of the aircraft and walking across the tarmac.

Magnusson, the mink-breeding, cigar-smoking, trawler-owning Communist, smiled glossily. 'Do you see your friend?'

'Not yet.'

'I am very interested in the study of volcanic activity.'

'Are you,' I said, flattening my voice with total disinterest.

'Did you know that there is volcanic activity under the American base? Right here, in fact.'

I said I had heard about it.

'You can imagine what the Russians in Reykjavik think

and dream about.' He finished his coffee with a couple of kitten sips. 'All these Americans here and all that activity underneath them.'

I smiled thinly, drumming my fingers on the table. 'I can imagine,' I said.

The last passenger had disembarked. Two stewardesses in scarlet walked prettily towards us. Neither possessed the unmistakeable contours of Gudrun.

'As a matter of fact,' Magnusson said, 'those three men over there are Russians. I meet them a lot in the fishing business.'

There were two of them, trying very hard to live up to the Western cartoonist conception of Russians. Square shoulders, wide trousers, hats perched rather than worn, faces waiting for winter. I wondered who they were meeting.

Then I saw Gudrun striding across the tarmac. The breeze was teasing her wings of hair and her chest swung slightly with the energy of her stride.

Magnusson stood up. 'Your friend will be joining you soon,' he said. 'I will leave you now. I hope that we will meet again very soon. Please remember that my home is yours.'

Which was overdoing it a bit, I thought, even for an Icelander.

We shook hands and I felt the dormant power of the man. From an inside pocket he took a small box – the sort that they sell cufflinks in. 'Please,' he said, 'a present for your . . . acquaintance.' He pressed the box into my hand and walked swiftly away.

I opened the box. It contained two mink earrings. Icelandic mink presumably. Or Russian.

'I am looking very much forward to making the love,' Gudrun said.

'So am I.'

'You do not sound wery enthusiastic,' she said in a pouting voice.

I squeezed her thigh reassuringly and took another look at the Mercedes that was following us. There wasn't much you could do about a tail on the long straight road across the lava field from the airport. The driver wore a peaked cap and there was someone sitting behind him – I couldn't see who. Magnusson perhaps? I accelerated but the distance between the two cars remained the same.

'I have bought you a present,' Gudrun said. She rustled around in her shoulder-bag.

'What is it?'

'It is a telescope for you to watch your birds with.'

'That was very sweet of you. Did it cost a lot of money?'

'Yesh,' she said. 'It cost much money.'

'I'll make it up to you,' I said, 'when we get back to your apartment.'

She brightened up. 'All the time we were flying I was thinking about making the love.'

I wondered what sort of service the passengers had received. 'Is that telescope very powerful?'

'Yesh,' she said. 'It is very powerful. It was the most powerful one in the shop.'

'Have you looked through it?'

'I looked through it in the plane.'

Which must have been rather disconcerting for the passengers. As if the captain had deputed her to try and find Iceland.

'I'd like to have a look,' I said.

'Then let us stop the car.'

'No, I want to get back to your apartment as soon as possible.'

She sighed contentedly. 'Then have a quick little look while you are driving. But do not have an accident.'

'Okay,' I said. 'Focus it for me. Try it out on that car behind otherwise you will only be looking at lava.'

'Wery vell.' She untelescoped the telescope, swivelled round in the seat and peered at the Mercedes.

And, because it would look very much to the chauffeur as if Gudrun were aiming a rifle right between his eyes, I waited expectantly.

The Mercedes swung across the path of an oncoming lorry and stopped at the roadside. The lorry also stopped abruptly, tyres screeching on the road. The driver climbed out and addressed himself to the chauffeur with vigour.

I stopped the Chevrolet and took the telescope from Gudrun.

'What is happening?' she asked. 'Why did that car behave like that when I tried to look at the driver?'

'He must have been shy,' I said.

I focused the telescope on the passenger in the back of the Mercedes. It was Jefferey. His face looked pained as he listened to the comments of the lorry driver.

I gave the telescope back to Gudrun and accelerated towards Reykjavik to make the love.

The love was made, the cigarettes were alight and we were playing word games. But not for long because there wasn't much time and there was a lot to do although I wasn't sure what.

Gudrun said: 'Do you know what the longest word in our language is?' She was lying naked on her stomach on the bed.

'No,' I said, with minimal interest. 'Then I will show you.'

She fetched pencil and paper, bouncing considerably as she walked, and wrote: *Haestarjettarmalaflutunesmanskifstofust ulkonutidyralykill*. That's using your letters,' she said. 'There are fifty-seven of them.'

'What does it mean?'

'It means the latchkey belonging to a girl working in the office of a barrister.'

'A phrase which you use frequently?'

'Not so frequently.'

'What about the latchkey *ring* belonging to a girl working in the office of a barrister?'

She considered this with displeasure. Then said: 'Yes, that is also possible.'

'Then it must be an even longer word.'

'I suppose so.' She brightened. 'You see what a wonderful language it is.'

'Yes,' I said, stroking her buttocks, moving up her spine and back again. Her hair smelled of lemon and her body of Johnson's baby powder.

She turned on her back and said: 'I think I love you, Bill.'

'Only think?'

'It is very difficult. Soon you will be gone. It is bad perhaps for me to love you.'

'I shall only go back to London. You fly into London a lot.'

'That would be worse than being in love with a pilot.'

'You sound something of an authority on it.'

She shrugged. 'I have flown with our pilots to foreign countries. I know how they behave. I would not like to be married to one.'

'Would you like me to stay in Iceland?'

'Yesh,' she said. 'Absolutely. I would like it.'

You could never accuse Gudrun of being devious. And maybe it wouldn't be such a bad idea at that. A job as interpreter, William Conransson, life close to the fire and the ice . . .

I pulled my trousers on and walked to the window. Metallic sea, clean air, black, sugared mountains and the wild stirring land beyond. Maybe it was a good idea. If I could first help to protect it from the infections of power politics.

'Bill,' she said.

'Yes?'

'Something is bothering you. I don't understand what it is. Is it because that American scientist you were meeting didn't arrive? Or is it that you are upset that I said I love you?'

I had forgotten the fictitious scientist I was supposed to have been meeting the day I arrived. 'Neither,' I said. 'The scientist is coming later and you only said you thought you loved me.'

'Now you play word games when they are not games any more.'

'Nothing is bothering me.' I waited for her to ask if I loved her; but she didn't.

'Come here,' she said. 'Forget whatever it is that is bothering you.'

I was half way through forgetting when there was a knock at the door.

I raised myself on one elbow and shouted: 'You'll have to wait, Jefferey. I'm busy.'

14

Jefferey

The club was one block from Gudrun's apartment. Downstairs consisted of a cloakroom and a large dark bar in which seamen in soap-pressed suits drank themselves into lurching stupidity with sombre dedication. They drank vodka and brandy and whisky as long drinks; and no one drank or even mentioned the pale beer.

The dancing and the girls were upstairs. Girls of all ages and sizes; dances of every vintage from something that looked like The Lancers, through to the Black Bottom and on to the Frug. The girls were very patient with their drunken, lecherous, homesick men and allowed themselves to be hugged, propelled and wept upon with equanimity. Some of the men were in their sixties and seventies, resurrecting the frolics of their youth with surprising agility.

There were a couple of youths on electric guitars, a drummer, someone on trumpet or sax, and a girl who looked as if she might be English singing *Daughter of Darkness* as we walked in.

'Why in God's name did we have to come to a place like this?' Jefferey asked.

'We didn't. We didn't have to come anywhere. I didn't have to drink with you at all – it was you who wanted this urgent chat.'

We sat at a table overlooking the dance floor. The other occupants were a kittenish girl with short, bleached hair and a mature lady with hairy legs.

Jefferey said: 'This is supposed to be confidential.'

'They won't understand what you're jabbering about.' I addressed the girl. 'Do you speak English?'

'Just a little,' she said; which meant a dozen or so words for bargaining with clients.

'And you?'

The older woman beamed horribly and moved closer to Jefferey.

I said to Jefferey: 'Fire away, old boy. And buy mama here a drink.'

Jefferey looked as if he might vomit; but he often looked like that. A waiter asked in English what we wanted to drink – he didn't seem to have any trouble in establishing Jefferey's nationality.

'I'll have a Scotch,' I said. 'A large one. And you ladies?'

They both giggled and ordered large vodkas. 'Don't forget yourself,' I said to Jefferey.

He ordered himself a small Scotch and said: 'I suppose you think this is bloody funny.'

'It's not without its moments.' I nodded towards his neighbour. 'Look out, old man, I think she's trying to undo your trousers.'

He moved away, brushing at her hand as if it were a mosquito. 'The situation in Iceland is getting pretty tense,' he said. 'This girl and the airman they're holding at Keflavik. And all this trouble over Hafstein. Do you realise that they hardly know the meaning of murder in this country?'

'There hasn't been a murder,' I said. 'Hafstein was shot by an Icelandic policeman and the girl choked herself to death.'

'Nevertheless the situation is very grave.' He leaned forward and I could smell a faint hyacinth scent on his glossy hair. 'We want to keep out of it as much as possible.'

'We?'

'Britain,' he breathed.

'Would you like to dance?' I said to the girl with the short yellow hair. As we walked to the dance floor the older woman was staring meaningfully at Jefferey.

The girl was stocky but light on her feet, having spent her adult life dodging sailors' sea-legs. She said: 'My name is Anna. What is your name?'

'Charlie,' I said.

'I like the name Charlie.'

The girl on the platform was singing *Raindrops keep falling on my head*. My partner moulded her thick little body with mine; her yellow hair was dark at the roots, her stomach felt hard; she managed to slide one leg in between mine with adroit professionalism. Beside us a drunk young seaman was dancing in slow-motion a few feet away from a pretty girl in pigtails; his arms flailed ponderously knocking a bottle off a table. He winked an apology, belched painfully and sat down on the floor, waiting to be hauled away. An old sea-dog jogged around with a woman in her fifties; they smiled happily at each other and she caressed the grey stubble at the back of his neck with a strong hand.

When we returned to the table Jefferey had shed his diplomatic training. His face and voice were petulant; his partner had gone.

'Where's mama gone?'

'I told her to piss off. Now look here, Conran – this is serious You don't realise just how serious. But it affects you. That's why I came round to see you. At least you can have the bloody decency to listen to what I've got to say.'

'I'm listening,' I said. The usual lock of hair had fallen across his damp forehead. His grey suit with its elegant lapels and his Brigade of Guards tie did not blend happily with the surroundings.

'Can't you get rid of that bloody girl?'

'Hey,' I said. 'What's happened to all that education on how to behave in Moscow and Washington?'

'This isn't Moscow or Washington and you aren't Brezhnev or Nixon. Now get rid of that girl. If you don't, I will.'

The girl looked unhappily at us. We were all saved by a middle-aged seaman wearing a navy-blue sweater and grey slacks. He asked if we would mind if he danced with her. Jefferey said: 'For God's sake take her away.' The seaman looked puzzled. I nodded at him and squeezed the girl's wrist.

'Right,' Jefferey said. 'Now I want to know what the hell you think you're up to?'

'Do you?' I said.

'You cocked everything up in Moscow. Now you seem hell-bent on doing the same thing in Iceland. Are you out of your mind poking an Icelandic girl while you're on this sort of mission?'

'I would be out of my mind if I didn't.' Anger spurted like a splash of acid inside me. I contemplated throwing the dregs of my Scotch in his face, or punching him straight on his aquiline nose. 'You know, Jefferey, I feel sorry for you. You will never be able to enjoy yourself no matter where you are or who you're with. You've been trained not to. I think it's rather sad.'

'Are you mixed up in this business of the dead girl?'

'I wanted to try and save the airman from being crucified. But there's nothing I can do. I know that now. That's why I've got time to have a drink with you.' I pushed my empty glass across the table. 'I'll have another large Scotch, please.'

Before Jefferey could protest a lurking waiter whipped the empty glasses over to the bar.

Jefferey said: 'The death of that girl is none of your bloody business. Just keep your nose out of it. Leave it to the Americans – it's their pigeon.'

'Do you want me to convey that message to Commander Martz?'

'Just stop stirring up trouble. Britain has established itself very nicely here after all that trouble about fishing rights. We can't afford to get ourselves involved in other people's troubles.'

'I rather thought we were all members of NATO. What's the matter, Jefferey? Does this sort of thing interfere with your bridge evenings and dinner parties with H.E.?'

A young Icelandic seaman sat down beside us and said: 'My name is Harald and my father is an archbishop.' Perhaps he had been drinking the altar wine. 'Are you American?'

Jefferey looked indignant and flapped his Guards tie with one finger. 'No; he said. 'We're English and we're very busy at the moment.'

The archbishop's son was delighted. 'Ah, good evenings, Englishmen. I like Englishmen. My father have many fights with you Englishmen over cod and he say he like Englishmen wery much.'

'For God's sake,' Jefferey said.

'Yes,' the seaman said. 'That is right – my father is an archbishop.'

'Don't be rude to him,' I said to Jefferey. 'He likes Englishmen. You want things kept like that, as I understand it.'

Jefferey leaned across the table to speak to the seaman. 'Excuse me,' he said. 'But we *are* having rather an important discussion.'

The young seaman beamed. 'I will have a wodka,' he said. And added confidentially: 'I like your Scotch whisky wery much. But I also like the wodka. Sometimes I have the two of them mixed.'

'Let's go to the bar,' Jefferey said. 'I haven't finished what I want to say. It's very important.'

The seaman said: 'After here we will go round the corner and have our drinks in a teapot.'

The prospect was intriguing. 'Why in a teapot?' I asked.

'Because they do not allow you to drink liquors. But if it is in the teapot they don't mind. A lot of us have our liquors in the teapot.' He blessed us with a choirboy smile. 'A lady plays the violin there too. '

The band swung into an old-fashioned waltz and several ladies whose way of life was far from old-fashioned were being swung dizzily round the floor. It was all very good-natured.

Suddenly the primate's son stood up and said: 'Now I have the dance. Then I shall see you over the teapots.' He grabbed a plain and grateful girl and pulled her into the mêlée.

I took my drink from the waiter and waited for Jefferey to pay. 'Clearly,' I said, 'you've been sent here by someone. Otherwise you wouldn't be putting up with all this. Now let me ask a few questions. Why the hell were you following me in that Mercedes from Keflavik?'

Jefferey reached for the remaining tatters of his training and said in his old bored voice: '*Absit ividia*. I wasn't following you, old boy, I wanted to speak to you at the airport but you were with that awful fellow Magnusson all the time. Then your dolly-bird turned up.'

'You should tell your driver to learn the difference between a telescope and a rifle.'

'Very droll,' he said. 'But there wasn't the slightest need to follow you because I knew exactly where you would go.'

'You make it sound as if I were going to a brothel.'

'Well?'

I tossed the whisky into his face. He dried his face with a folded white handkerchief and searched for the ice inside his jacket. Now all his training had evaporated because it didn't embrace such behaviour. 'That was a shitty thing to do,' he said.

'That was a shitty thing to say.'

No one took much notice of us.

Jefferey said: 'It's just the sort of behaviour I would expect from a creep like you.' He took a piece of melting ice from inside his shirt. 'I'm pleased to say that I have some extremely bad news for you.'

'You mean we're going to see each other again?'

He took a tiny comb from his breast pocket and combed the front of his hair, now pomaded with Scotch.

'Worse even than that,' he said.

'What could possibly be worse?'

'The Russians are on to you, old man. That's what.'

He enjoyed my consternation with schoolboy pleasure. I could tell from his suppressed eagerness that there was more to come. He was so absorbed with the effect of his statement that I thought he might even buy another drink to replace the one I had thrown over him.

'What Russians?' I said. 'What are you talking about?'

'You've been recognised, old boy. Spotted, rumbled. Someone who knew about your little contretemps in Moscow must be over here.' He almost giggled. 'Perhaps all Russian diplomats were issued with those photographs.'

'And perhaps you would like a punch in the mouth?'

But no crude threats could spoil his pleasure. 'That's why I had to see you. H.E. is treating it very seriously.'

'Is he?' I said. 'You realise of course that I don't come under the jurisdiction of the Ambassador?'

'You jolly soon come running to the embassy if you get into trouble as I recall it. '

'How do you know that the Russians are "on to me"?'

'I am not at liberty to disclose that.'

I pulled his tie into a tight knot like a Brussels sprout 'I give you your liberty. How do you know the Russians are "on to me"?'

'It was at a lunch given today for the delegates to that marine conference. One of the Russian diplomats made it his business to let me know that you had been identified.'

'Are you sure you didn't let them know?'

'I'm not that stupid. I don't like you but I put my country before personal considerations.' He removed my hand from his tie; his grip was surprisingly strong.

The archbishop's son reappeared and asked if we were going round the corner to drink out of a teapot. We said we weren't.

'All right.' I said. 'So the Russians know who I am. So what? Nothing was ever proved against me in Moscow. Nothing political, that is. I have to pop up somewhere, don't I? Why not Iceland? My cover in Russia was scientific: my cover here is scientific. What the hell does it matter if the Russians have identified me? If I materialised in Mauritius they might recognise me. And, let's face it, someone was aware of the purpose of my visit before I'd even boarded the plane at London Airport. They did, after all, take a pot shot at me the evening I arrived. So, you see, it's not so much a question of me being recognised. It's a question of whether they know whom I suspect. And at the moment I think they've got it all wrong.' I sat back and beckoned the waiter. 'So you see, Jefferey old son, it doesn't really matter a monkey's toss whether or not the Russians have recognised me. Sorry to disappoint you and all that.'

'That isn't quite the way they see it at the embassy.'

I was so pleased with my spiel that I bought Jefferey a drink. 'To hell with the embassy,' I said.

'No one was very pleased when they heard you were coming in the first place.'

'I bet they weren't – not after you'd had your little say. Did you show them the photographs?'

He fiddled with the knot in his tie. 'They thought you were a bit of a security risk.'

'So are the Russians being infiltrated into this country?'

A girl in a trouser suit with a neckline down to her navel asked us for a light. Jefferey obliged, trying not to look at her chest and succeeding in looking furtive. 'You dance?' she said.

'No thanks,' he said. 'Not just now.' He smiled politely.

I said: 'In any case, why the urgency? Couldn't it have waited until tomorrow?'

'We'll all be very busy tomorrow. Their National day and everything. We have to show the flag.'

'What's wrong with the day after?'

'We wanted to be sure that you understood if you were recalled.'

I put down my glass and stared at Jefferey. He patted his shiny hair and stared back. He wasn't the one to dodge a fray. 'Just what the bloody hell are you talking about now?'

'We sent a message back to the F.O. when we heard that the Russians were on to you. Obviously they had to know. I expect you'll be getting a cable or something soon recalling you. Despite what you say you can't continue to operate once your front has been blown. You'd be followed every-where. And in any case it wouldn't help us at the embassy if the Russians thought we'd brought an agent in.'

'That's really it, isn't it?' I said. 'You don't want to be embarrassed. You've got over your little cod war and now you don't want any more bloody trouble. You don't want the Russians complaining to the Icelandic Government that we're spying on them. You don't want me nosing about in the investigation into this girl's death irrespective of whether it had anything to do with my assignment or not. And you certainly don't want a fellow who's been photographed in bed with a Russian bird around the place. It's all too much for your cosy little set-up, isn't it, Jefferey? And now you've found a way to get rid of me. Well, just don't count on it, my fine friend. Don't count on it at all. H.E. is not my boss and you. are most certainly my subordinate.'

'Just the same,' Jefferey said, 'I think you'll be leaving here pretty soon.' He smiled. '*Nil desperandum.*'

'You make me sick,' I said. 'Do you know that? Physically sick. The Russians have got you all just where they want you and you can't see it.'

'I'm already acquainted with your views on the British Diplomatic service,' Jefferey said. He was really enjoying himself.

'The Hammer and Sickle have only got to be raised a fraction of an inch and you're all hopping around like blue-arsed flies. Don't you realise that there are more important things at stake than keeping the embassy out of trouble? Don't you realise that this girl's death and the people I'm investigating are all part of a plan to end Western dominance here? To bring the Americans into disrepute, ultimately to get rid of NATO. Don't you realise that you're just playing into their hands – as always? They know that I'm on to something, they know I constitute a threat, so they bleat to you about it.'

'Aren't you rather overestimating your importance, old man?'

'If it wasn't me it would have been another agent. They would have bleated about him and you would have said "yes sir, sorry sir, three bags full, sir".'

'It doesn't matter, really, does it?' Jefferey buttoned his jacket, straightened his tie and combed at the hair about his ears with his fingers: his departure, he was telling me, was imminent.

'What do you mean, it doesn't matter?'

'You'll be able to brief your successor, won't you, old man?'

'Then the Russians will protest about his arrival and you'll cable the F.O. again and everything will be back to square one.'

'I rather think not,' he said, waiting for me to ask why not.

'Why not?' I said.

'I rather think I might be taking over,' he said.

He had to be joking. Surely they hadn't sunk to this.

He enjoyed his triumph for a few moments, then let it fade. Now he wanted to be taken seriously, wanted to conspire. He decided not to leave and looked around with theatrical caution before speaking.

One of the guitarists was singing *Wandrin' Star* in a fair imitation of Lee Marvin. Slivers of light through the curtains reminded us that night was day in Iceland.

Jefferey said: 'Can I get you another drink?'

'Yes,' I said.

Then he said: 'No one thinks that you've made any wrong moves in this assignment. It's just bad luck that the Russians have spotted you.' He searched for acceptable words. 'It seems that I'm the only possible successor because no one else at the F.O. has good enough Icelandic.'

'What about the night watchman at the embassy?'

The drinks came and Jefferey paid for them. Some of the girls still waiting for partners looked at us with puzzlement mingled with resentment. If we were queer what were we doing here?

Jefferey said: 'Of course, I will have to have your assessment of the situation here.' I was pleased to see that the whisky had left a light stain on his shirt.

'Of course,' I said.

He looked furtively around again like a drug pedlar. 'What part did Hafstein play in all this?'

'I don't know,' I said with refreshing honesty.

'Come on, Conran. You must know. After all you followed him to the Westman Islands and you were there when he died.' He paused to consolidate his position. 'Look here, we've got to work together on this. After all, the issues involved are far greater than private animosity. Surely you will agree with that?'

'It's a question of priorities,' I said. 'Certainly the issues involved are more important than us bickering. But what I have to decide is this: Would it be more disastrous for the Western Alliance to give you information or to withhold it? In my opinion it would be more disastrous to give it to you. In fact it would be catastrophic.'

His handsome face tightened. 'In that case I shall have to request your people in London to order you to hand it over.'

'You can try,' I said. 'As far as I'm concerned I'm still working here until I hear to the contrary.' I finished my drink. 'And I have no intention whatsoever, now or at any other time, of handing over any information to an amateur.'

'One wishes your competence matched your arrogance,' he said. 'I was in Chancery in Moscow, you know. And I was attached to intelligence in the Army.'

'God save us,' I said.

'So you won't co-operate?'

'Right.'

'You consider your own aspirations to be more important than curbing the Russian menace?'

'You're more naïve than anyone has any right to be. Do you realise I have no confirmation whatsoever of anything you've told me? Do you realise that you're asking me to hand over secret information just because you tell me that the Russians are wise to me and that London will probably recall me?' I sighed. 'Jefferey, old son, get the bum-fluff shaved off your cheeks.'

They were dancing now to *Strangers in the Night*. Staggering, cuddling, caressing, propositioning. The women had all given us up as a bad English joke.

Jefferey said: 'What does *German Church* mean?'

'Who the hell told you about that?'

'It doesn't matter who told me. What does it mean?'

'Ask me another.' I thought about it. 'I suppose that scientist told you?'

'He did as it happens. What does it mean?'

'I haven't the faintest idea.'

'Then I shall have to send a message to London asking them to expedite instructions to you.'

'Sometimes,' I said, 'you sound as if you're reading from a manual. Anyway, off you go to report back to His Excellency or whoever has the misfortune to receive your reports. And watch for the bullets as you drive past Stapi.'

We walked out into the bright evening. Two men were having a fight, watched with desultory interest by some youths and a couple of taxi drivers.

Jefferey had brought his own car this time. A red, hardtop MG which didn't somehow partner his pin-stripe and suede shoes.

He took off at great speed, turning a corner with squealing tyres, just missing an old woman carrying a basket of fish. Surely the Foreign Office was jesting?

I walked back to Gudrun's apartment. She mixed me a weak whisky and said: 'Perhaps you have had enough to drink already?'

'Perhaps,' I said, sipping it.

'Bill,' she said, making a business of lighting a cigarette and then staring across the bay at the crumpled mountains.

'Yes?'

'I have some bad news for you.'

Jesus, I thought – I shall always remember the eve of Iceland's National day. 'How bad?'

'Oh, not very bad. Just a temporary badness.' She sat on the arm of the chair. 'Do you love me, Bill?'

I made a vague motion with my head and mumbled into my Scotch. She waited until I couldn't decently hold the glass to my lips any longer and said: 'Do you?'

'I'm very fond of you.' How many times had that escape route been used?

'Only fond?'

'More than fond.'

'How fond?'

There wasn't really much you could do about Icelandic girls. 'Okay,' I said, 'I love you.' I could understand why some girls preferred Latin lovers. 'Now, what's the bad news?'

'Johann has come back from the sea.'

She made it sound as if he had come back from the dead.

'So you want me to leave?'

'Just for two hours. That's all. I want to explain to him what has happened.' She stroked my cheek. 'Then you can return and we will make the love again.'

'All right,' I said. 'But do me one favour.'

'What is that?'

'Don't give him my address.'

I was about to be relieved of my assignment, Shirey would be handed over and I was powerless to intervene . . . all I needed was a punch-up with a brawny fisherman in my boarding house and the landlady smelling my breath.

Gudrun kissed me. 'Come back at midnight,' she said. 'I will be waiting.'

I walked to the cab rank outside the bar. The two men were still fighting. As I walked past, the mature lady who had been sitting at our table came out and waved delightedly at me. I jumped in a cab and told the driver to take me into town.

15

The London End

There was a message at Baragata that there was a cable for me awaiting collection. A recall? Whatever happened I wouldn't hand anything over to Jefferey. For the sake of world peace.

My landlady met me on the way out. 'Soon,' she said, 'it will be our National day. I am so pleased that you will be here.'

'I'm pleased, too,' I said.

'There will be processions and amusements and much dancing in the parks. You will dance in the parks?' she said, as if she were asking me for the first waltz.

'I am a little old for dancing in parks,' I said.

'You are not old, Mr Conran. You are young. Many womens would like to dance with you.'

'Why, thank you,' I said.

'We have many good vacations here. You would like the ninth day of October for instance. In Reykjavik we celebrate the day Leif Ericsson discovered North America and we pay homage at his statue.'

'Do the Russians pay homage?'

She smiled vaguely. 'I do not know, Mr Conran. Should they?'

'They should,' I said, 'because I don't know what they would do with themselves if someone hadn't discovered it.'

I walked briskly through the toytown streets to the cable office where they had instructions to hold any cables for me. But it wasn't a recall: it was a cable telling me that there was a courier at the Hotel Borg with a dispatch for me.

I walked across the square to the Borg and asked for Mr Willard.

Mr Willard presented himself at reception with an envelope cunningly concealed in a newspaper. He was a worried-looking man in a baggy, expensive suit – like a bank manager with too many overdrafts. He handed me the envelope in the toilet, then waited and worried.

He said he wouldn't have a drink and rather thought he would have an early night. I signed for the envelope, recommended the valet service for pressing his suit and went to the bar. It was 10 p.m. – two hours to Shirey's deadline.

There were a couple of young men at the bar. Shaggy hair, bell-bottomed corduroy slacks and pendants hanging at their chests. The uniform of protest – or drugged defeat. They were away from their territory because the bar was usually inhabited by businessmen or tourists.

I ordered a Scotch. I felt a little drunk. The envelope crackled in my pocket but I was scared of taking it back to Baragata because I thought I knew what it contained. I smiled at the two young men because I liked their bravado. One of them smiled back and I said: 'Are you getting tanked up for tomorrow?' Or the Icelandic equivalent of that.

He said in English: 'Are you American?' He looked very self-conscious about his gear.

'No, British.'

That silenced them briefly because they had decided that I *was* American.

The other one rolled a cigarette and asked me for a light. Half the cigarette went up in flame, endangering his hair. 'What do you think about all this?' he asked.

'All what?'

'All this cover up by the Yanks about the girl?'

'I didn't know they were covering anything up.'

'Not covering up, perhaps.' He stared into his glass and blinked more slowly than I thought it possible to blink. 'Holding out on?' He looked at me hopefully.

'I didn't know they were holding out.'

His companion who wore a sweatshirt dyed mauve beneath a blue corduroy blouse said: 'Very soon we shall be marching on the base. We shall demand that the American murderer be handed over. If they do not hand him over then we shall enter the base and take him.' He pounded his chest carefully. 'We do not care if they shoot, we shall take him. Already we have penetrated their base and showed what we think of their television.'

'But you have American programmes on your own television, don't you?'

'That is quite different,' his friend said firmly. His sweatshirt was orange with a black skull-and-crossbones inked on the back. 'Will you march with us?'

'No,' I said. 'It's your march. I wouldn't want to spoil it. Are all the young people of Iceland taking part?'

'They will if it doesn't rain,' said mauve shirt.

The dispatch was in response to the cable I sent to London shortly after my arrival in Reykjavik. For a while it kept me in suspense with its bureaucratic formality. 'In reply to your di-da-di-da of the da-di-da.' Then I got down to the meat. My reading became slower in the whitewashed bedroom as I approached the information that I didn't want to know. But there was no escape; just as there hadn't been any escape from my divorce from the moment the Russian cameraman got me in focus.

'. . . in response to your request we arranged for the subject to be followed from London Airport. She went straight to her hotel with the rest of the crew. She was allotted Room 212. She stayed there for about an hour and made one telephone call which we intercepted. The call was to a friend of hers at the Icelandic Tourist Office in Piccadilly. The conversation was confined to female gossip during which the subject talked about meeting a wonderful Englishman who was staying in Reykjavik. Bracket, the operator intercepting the conversation took it upon himself to identify the Englishman as yourself, unbracket.'

I smiled and lay back on the bed for a moment. Outside I saw a group of youths walking towards the coach station carrying folded banners. I could just make out the word 'American' on one of the folds.

'After the phone call she was visited by the pilot of the aircraft . . .'

For how long? I thought. For how long did the lecherous, world-weary bastard touch down in Room 212?

'. . . He stayed only two minutes and left looking somewhat ill-tempered, according to a female operative who was working as a maid in the corridor at the time. The pilot subsequently called at the room of another stewardess where he was allowed to stay for approximately an hour. He left looking much happier . . .'

The author of the cable had a sense of humour, which was unusual.

'. . . The subject stayed in her room for another half hour during which time she asked Room Service to send her up a Club Sandwich and a glass of milk. She left one hour and thirty-five minutes after arrival and caught a bus to Hounslow. From there she caught the underground to High

Street Kensington. She had changed into civilian clothes'
– as if the red uniform put her on a war footing – 'and was
wearing a green costume and a silk headscarf with a leopard-
skin pattern . . .'

A man's description of fashion. But now we were
approaching the guts of it.

'. . . She went first to a coffee shop opposite the underground station. She had a cup of coffee and a Swedish
pastry. She read *Nova* magazine and appeared to acknow-
ledge the presence of a man who entered the coffee shop
by rolling up her magazine as if it were a pre-arranged
signal. Shortly after this she left the coffee shop. So did the
man. She walked down High Street Kensington in the
direction of Olympia. Our operative anticipated that she
would be picked up by some kind of vehicle and hired a
taxi. About 200 yards past the Odeon cinema another taxi
slowed down and stopped in front of her. She climbed in.
Our operative was able to identify the other passenger as
the man whom she had acknowledged in the coffee shop.

'The taxi proceeded in the direction of Olympia, then
doubled back along the High Street. Before reaching
Knightsbridge it turned into Kensington Gardens/Hyde Park
and emerged in Bayswater Road. It stopped outside a public
house in the Bayswater Road and the subject and her
companion went inside. After about fifteen minutes they
were joined by a man whom the operative identified as one
of the newcomers to the staff of the Russian Embassy . . .'

'*I'm very fond of you.*'
'*Only fond?*'
'*More than fond.*'
'*How fond?*'
'*Okay, I love you.*'

'. . . The three people under surveillance stayed together
for approximately twenty minutes during which time they
each consumed one whisky. At one stage the subject handed

over a large envelope which the representative of the
Russian Embassy put in his briefcase . . .'

The prying, prosaic message proceeded as inexorably and
regularly as a policeman's footsteps.

'Bill, there's something I must tell you.'

'Yes, what is it?'

'I want a divorce.'

'Is there someone else?'

'No. No one else. Just those damned photographs. Those damned,
damned photographs.'

' . . . The representative of the Russian Embassy left first.
Then the subject and her companion hailed another taxi.
The subject alighted in Piccadilly where she entered a shop
selling camera equipment and binoculars. She emerged with
a package. Bracket, a later check elicited the information
that she bought a telescope, unbracket. She then went to
Piccadilly Circus underground station and bought a ticket
to Hounslow. From Hounslow she caught a bus back to her
hotel . . .'

All I needed now, I thought, was the return of the pilot.

' . . . The rest of the aircraft's crew were having a party
in one of their rooms. They phoned her several times asking
her to join them but she declined on each occasion. At
11.30 p.m. she hung a Do Not Disturb notice on her door
and requested an early call at 7.30 a.m. on the telephone.
She did not come under direct surveillance again until 8.30
a.m. the following day when she came down to the restaurant for breakfast.'

And no doubt ate a hearty meal.

The report concluded with a timetable of her morning.
Lots of coffee, magazine reads, a drink at the bar, lunch,
preparations for the return flight.

The policeman's feet followed her to the airport and then
watched her on to the Boeing through binoculars.

The author of the report, who was proud of the operation,

said that photographs he had taken of the subject, her companion and the Russian, with a Minox camera were being studied. Also the drivers of the two taxis which the subject had used were being questioned to see if they overheard any conversation.

I burned the report and flushed the ash down the toilet. It seemed the best place for it.

Then I walked into the centre of town. A coach waited at the traffic lights outside the *Morgenbladid* offices. It was full of youths and girls with placards heading for the NATO base. Out at the base Shirey would be putting on his best uniform now to meet police, press and public.

I glanced at my watch. It was 11 p.m. It would soon be dusk or dawn – whichever way you looked at it. It would soon be Iceland's National day. Whoopee.

16

National Day

Her face was pale, her gossamer hair uncombed. She wore a white housecoat with green piping. She was smoking a cigarette.

'It's not midnight,' she said. 'We said midnight.'

'Where's Johann?'

I pushed her aside and went into the living room.

'He went. I told him about us.'

'Was his ship a Russian trawler?'

'No, Icelandic. Why do you ask?'

'Sit down,' I said.

'Bill, what is the matter?'

'Everything,' I said. 'Everything is the matter. Sit down there.' I pointed to a chair beside the table.

'You are acting very strangely. What is the matter? Why have you come so early?'

I lit a cigarette, contemplated the whisky bottle and decided against it: my self-pity needed no further lubricants. I sat opposite her.

I said: 'Your trouble, Gudrun, is that you're not a very good actress. You over-act.'

'I don't know what you're talking about.' The line was too familiar. I wondered if she would cry.

'You shouldn't have made the pick-up quite so obvious on the plane. I don't flatter myself, Gudrun. There wasn't any of this instant attraction at work: you were ordered to pick me up. But I didn't respond too well and you had to do a follow-up job at the airport.'

She shook her head miserably. 'I liked you. I wanted to meet you again. That's the way it is in Iceland.' She made an attempt at a smile. 'As I told you – brains first, then looks.'

'It's a pity about the brains,' I said. 'I have just a few, you see, otherwise I wouldn't have sent a cable to London.'

'What cable?'

'There are one or two things I would like to know,' I said. 'Among other things I would like to know if you have ever had any feeling for me.'

Her eyes seemed to moisten – but it might have been my imagination. 'I love you,' she said. 'I told you that.'

'Tell that to the Russian marines,' I said. Which wasn't very gallant.

The moisture intensified and two diamond tears took up positions at the corners of her eyes. 'You talk in puzzles.'

'I work in puzzles. It's odd to think that you've known about me all the time.'

'Known what about you?'

'Just about everything, I suppose. Did you know about Moscow? About the photographs?'

'I don't know anything about any photographs.'

I believed her because I wanted to.

'I sent a cable arranging for you to be followed in London,' I said.

The tears froze. Defeat aged her face. She got up and put on a record. Sandie Shaw and *There's Always Something There to Remind Me*. Too loud.

She said softly: 'You must go. Now. Quickly.'

'Why, is Johann coming back?'

'Now, please go. Someone else is coming.'

'You've got a lot to tell me first,' I said. 'First of all, tell me why?'

'There is no point. You wouldn't understand. I didn't understand . . .'

Even now I wanted her to say something that would permit forgiveness.

'What do you mean, you didn't understand?' There was a slight swelling on her lip which reminded me of the dead girl. 'You didn't understand that your friends were using that girl's death to create anti-American feeling? You didn't understand that a kid out at the base is going to have his life ruined because of your friends?'

The tears melted and slid down her cheeks. 'I didn't understand. I was just a Communist like many other young people in Iceland. It's not the same . . .'

'It *was* just the same with you,' I said. 'Just the same and worse.'

'Please go,' she said. 'I won't run away. Come back tomorrow.'

Sandie Shaw progressed on to *Long Live Love*. Still too loud. I turned down the volume. Gudrun blinked some more tears from her eyes. Her housecoat fell open giving me a glimpse of her breasts. She covered them with a listless movement. Outside a shower of rain crossed the bay, heading out to sea.

I said: 'I suppose you know someone tried to kill me shortly after we met?'

'Yesh,' she said. The lisp or whatever it was had lost some of its appeal.

'Did you arrange that?'

'No – they knew you were coming anyway.'

'But that didn't stop you, did it?' There really wasn't much she could say to encourage forgiveness.

'I only found out about the shooting today. I didn't know they had tried to kill you. They wouldn't have wanted me to know. They didn't tell me any of the bad things. I thought it was just a question of . . .'

'Ideology?'

'Yesh,' she said. 'Ideology like the students have. But they forget it so soon after they have finished their studies.'

I walked over to the window. Ideology. The cause of as much dishonesty, suffering and deceit as original sin. The sky was clear again, paling for the dusk-dawn. The mountains had advanced in the rain-washed clarity encircling the scattered roofs of Reykjavik. Beyond, the glaciers and volcanoes on the thin crust of the earth. Ideology!

In the street below a minibus packed with young people headed towards the base.

At the best Gudrun was stupid. At the best. But she had never appeared particularly stupid. Single-minded, unsubtle, hungry and healthy; but not stupid.

I looked at my watch. It was 11.30. In half an hour Shirey would be handed over. I could vaguely smell a familiar scent, but I couldn't place it.

I sat down again and gripped her wrist. 'Look, do you know anything that can save this boy out at the base?'

She shook her head, scattering a couple of tears on to the polished table-top.

I tightened my grip. 'You must know something. You were being used as a courier after all. A courier is a very important member of an organisation. What was in that envelope that you handed over to the Russian in a London pub yesterday?'

'I don't know,' she said. She was trembling and dabbing distractedly at the tears. 'I told you – I knew nothing. I didn't read the report.'

'Just in it for the ideology? Come on, Gudrun.' I let go of her wrist. 'In half an hour your country will be celebrating the day it was granted home rule by the Danes. Freedom in other words. You know what you're doing, Gudrun? You're helping people who want to end that freedom.'

She shrugged helplessly.

'What's that bruise on your lip?'

'It is nothing.'

'All right,' I said, 'we'll tackle it from another angle. I want to know the names of the people in Iceland for whom you were working. And for God's sake don't say you don't know who they were.'

'I cannot tell you,' she said.

'Please,' I said. 'Please tell me, Gudrun. If you don't then I shall have to hand you over to someone who will make you talk It's not very difficult, you know.'

'Then you must hand me over: I cannot tell you.'

Miss Shaw changed to a number called *I've Heard About Him* as if she were following our dialogue.

I said: 'If you won't tell me then I will give you some names.'

Fear animated her expression. She said urgently: 'No, you mustn't. Please.'

'Olav Magnusson,' I said.

'Please,' she said. 'Don't.'

'Valdimar Laxdal,' I said.

Valdimar Laxdal said: 'I can confirm that, Mr Conran.'

He was standing at the bedroom doorway, gun in hand held with love and familiarity. Now I identified the scent: it was Laxdal's aftershave.

'So this is Johann,' I said to Gudrun. I moved one hand in the general direction of my Smith & Wesson.

Laxdal jerked his gun. A Beretta: it would be – flash name like its owner. 'Hands firmly clasped behind your neck, please.'

'Did you kill the girl?' I asked.

'Let us say she died. No one killed her.'

'Wrong,' I said. 'Whoever fixed that date with Shirey killed her. Whoever filled her up with booze killed her. Whoever persuaded her that she was doing it for Iceland killed her. You killed her, Laxdal. You and whoever helped you.' I looked at Gudrun.

He leaned against the doorway. His pose was lazy, his grip on the gun firm. 'Does it matter? She was only a little tart.' He was speaking in English.

'Do you matter? You're only a little ponce.'

The actor's smile hardened fractionally. 'Gudrun, take Mr Conran's gun. It's inside his jacket.' To me he said: 'Don't try anything now because it will not bother me in the slightest if I shoot our mutual mistress as well as you.'

Gudrun stood the distance from me that her bosom required. The tears had stopped. She didn't look at me. She took the gun from the holster and said: 'I tried to warn you. I told you not to tell me any names.'

'Thanks,' I said.

Laxdal said: 'Put the gun on the table.' The dimple in his smooth chin looked very deep tonight. He was wearing blue slacks, light blue button-down shirt with a dark blue neckerchief and a casual suede jacket, expensive, probably French. The clothes were all a little too young for him. He looked freshly tanned, freshly combed, freshly exercised.

She put the Smith & Wesson on the table and sat down. Sandie Shaw sang *I'd Be Far Better Off Without You*.

'My arms are getting very tired,' I said. 'Very soon I shall have to let them drop. Then you will shoot me. I don't want that.'

'I shall have to kill you anyway,' Laxdal said. 'But not here. Not in this beautiful apartment where you found so much happiness with Gudrun.'

'Jealous?' I said. 'You shouldn't be. After all, it was you

who ordered her to pick me up. You or Magnusson. To pick my brains, I suppose. She didn't produce many pickings, did she, Laxdal? '

'She would have done.' He wasn't enjoying this particular reality. 'She would have started tonight. In the post-coital sadness – isn't that when men are supposed to give up their secrets?'

'I wouldn't know,' I said. 'I've never been very sad after coitus.' Nor, I thought, have you – you've just read that somewhere.

Laxdal said: 'All right, sit down in that chair.' He pointed to a Swedish easy-chair, white and shallow and uncomfortable. 'Keep your hands on the arms. Don't try anything because I am a very good shot and very fast.'

'And very proud of it,' I said. He gestured with the gun, a bad-tempered jerk. I sat down.

'There are some details I should like to know,' he said.

'And me. When did you come to Iceland, Laxdal? Are you Russian or are you just an Icelandic traitor?'

Gudrun said: 'He is a murderer.' She was sitting at the table feeling the bruise on her lip.

'And who's the boss,' I said. 'You or Magnusson?' I knew he would answer that one.

'I am.' He sat down opposite me, one hand instinctively tugging at his trousers to preserve the crease. 'What interests me is your interest in Hafstein.'

'He was a suspect. Just like you and Magnusson. He doesn't matter very much now, does he?'

'He matters,' Laxdal said. 'He matters because he wasn't working for me and he wasn't working for you. Who was he working for and what sort of set-up did he have? I need to know that, Conran. I need to know it very badly. And I need to know it before you die. As you just observed to Gudrun, a man or a woman can always be made to talk. There is no such thing any longer as resistance to persuasion.'

'You can persuade all you wish but you won't get anything from me because I don't know the answer to your question.'

Laxdal lit a *Gauloise* very carefully and the gun-barrel didn't waver. 'Why did you suspect him?'

'Because of your agent who was shot dead at Egilsstathir.'

'What about him?'

'He had a scrap of paper in his pocket with Hafstein's name on it.'

Laxdal considered this and detached a shred of black tobacco from his tongue.

'You don't like that, do you, Laxdal? It smells of a plot within a plot, doesn't it? A Russian agent with instructions to report to someone other than yourself. You know what I think? I think that your days here in charge of operations were numbered. I think Hafstein was working for your Kremlin masters without your knowledge. He may even have been senior to you. Perhaps you've been indiscreet, Laxdal. Men of your age and conceit are given to boasts that are inclined to be indiscreet. In any case you're not the type the Soviet system warms to: they don't like ageing playboys. They use them – as they used Philby for instance – then discard them or put them out to graze. Philby was lucky – if you call being a prisoner in Moscow lucky. But you aren't as important or as well-known as Philby. They wouldn't even bother to discard you, Laxdal – they would dispose of you. Perhaps that was the mission of the unfortunate agent who got himself shot by a wandering policeman. Perhaps even now another agent has been landed, without your knowledge, to dispose of you.'

A black and white ship edged into the picture framed by the window. Five miles away, perhaps, but you could still pick out the national flag – red cross bordered with white on a dark blue background. There were flags everywhere. In twenty minutes Shirey would be handed over.

Laxdal inhaled the smell of France deeply. His gun was still steady but his face had creased up a bit. Valdimar Laxdal did not enjoy being belittled in front of a woman. 'You can keep your theories,' he said. 'All I want to know is what you found out about Hafstein.'

'I told you – nothing. He was an enthusiastic and competent ornithologist and a lover of Icelandic churches. He was particularly fond' – I watched Laxdal's reactions closely – 'of a certain German church.'

The reactions were non-existent. Laxdal said: 'You are wasting time.'

I shrugged. One brief phone call to Martz and Shirey would be saved. The demonstrators would be assembled now outside the base. Young and eager, finding strength and hatred in their numbers. Taking their lessons from the students of Paris, London, Tokyo, New York. The trouble in Iceland was that there was little to protest about. So you picked on the Americans. And if your protest succeeded and the Americans went and the Russians arrived then no one would ever be allowed to protest again . . .

The Smith & Wesson lay on the table about five feet away. Laxdal intercepted my thoughts. 'Don't,' he said. 'Stay alive for a little while. Now tell me about Hafstein. The truth.' His aftershave smelled stronger now as if suppressed emotion were releasing it.

Gudrun said: 'May I go and lie down?'

Laxdal said: 'No.' He squashed the *Gauloise* butt on the carpet with his foot. 'Why did Hafstein make a run for it? You must have discovered something or else he would not have tried to escape.'

'Your guess,' I said, 'is as good as mine.'

'No guesses, Mr Conran. Just facts, please. Why did he make a break for it?'

'Perhaps he was "regrouping". Doesn't it strike you as odd that he should flee to the Westman Islands where

Magnusson had a house? Isn't it possible that Magnusson and he were about to execute a coup within the Russian espionage network in Iceland?' I managed the bantering sort of smile that you're supposed to manage in such circumstances. 'Are you so sure, Laxdal, that Magnusson was really your subordinate? He doesn't strike me as the sort of person who would willingly be subordinate to anyone.'

It was good thinking material and Laxdal thought about it.

I pushed on with my luck. 'Did you know that Magnusson was at Keflavik airport when I went out there to meet Gudrun?'

'No,' he said. 'What of it?'

'Nothing – except that I think he went to meet three Russians there. They were standing around looking like spare parts at a wedding pretending they were meeting someone off the plane. But they didn't meet anyone. I'm pretty sure they had arranged a meeting with Magnusson. But when Magnusson saw me he didn't go through with it.'

'Why the hell would they choose Keflavik airport for a secret meeting?'

Why the hell would they? 'I don't know,' I said. 'But from your point of view, Laxdal, it's worth pursuing. Especially as Magnusson doesn't seem to have told you that he met me there.'

A crease made itself known between Laxdal's nose and the corner of his mouth. He rippled his blond hair with his free hand.

He said: 'Are you going to tell me the truth about Hafstein?'

'I've told you all I know. But as you won't believe me you'd better get on with whatever you're going to do. Incidentally,' I added, 'why did you hit Gudrun?'

'She asked for it. Just as you are asking for it.'

Gudrun said: 'I found out the truth about the girl. And I said I couldn't get any information from you.'

Which was hardly surprising because she hadn't really tried – apart from asking me if Hekla was my only reason for being in Iceland. But she had known the answer to that anyway.

Laxdal said: 'So you're not going to tell me?'

I said I wasn't.

'Then I shall have to persuade you. To tell the truth I would prefer to beat the facts out of you. And make no mistake – I would succeed. But you are an experienced agent, quite tough in your own strange way.' If bird watchers *can* be tough, he implied. 'You would last quite a time. With a drug I will have the truth in five minutes. You know that, Mr Conran. Why not save us both the trouble?'

'If I could I would,' I said.

'Stand up,' he said. I stood up. 'Turn round.' I turned round.

'I shall knock you out now,' he said. 'Scientifically. It will hardly hurt and you will be unconscious for about five minutes. When you regain consciousness you will be strapped down on the bed and I shall give you an injection.'

No point in ducking or swivelling or back-kicking. Not with a man like Laxdal. I waited for the blow that would paralyse the nerves.

The blast was hot and loud, astonishing the senses. For a fraction of a moment I thought it was the blow. But I was still standing and the black and white ship had moved into the centre of the picture.

I turned round. Laxdal was folding up, one hand still holding the Beretta, the other feeling for the mess of blood and splintered bone that had been his face.

Gudrun's finger was still tight round the trigger of the Smith & Wesson and Sandie Shaw was singing *I'll Stop at Nothing*.

I picked up the phone and dialled 24324. They took a hell of a long time finding Martz – about thirty seconds, probably. It was 11.55.

He said: 'Yes, who is it?'

'It's me,' I said. 'Conran.'

He said: 'Sorry Bill, old buddy. No dice.'

'Oh yes,' I said. 'There is dice. We've got the man responsible for the girl's death.'

It took me another minute to persuade him not to hand Shirey over.

In the apartment the needle ran off the track of *The Golden Hits of Sandie Shaw*.

17

Gudrun

The sky was ice-blue and the lake took its colour from it. The plain was grey and mauve and the sedge at the shores of the lake took its colour from the plain. White mountains hovered on the perimeter of the plain and one cone was reflected in the still water. Somewhere in the lava field I could hear water flowing.

Thingvellir. The plain where the forerunner of the Icelandic Parliament was first established in 930. Virtually nothing remains of the original buildings; but, as the guide-book says, it is 'the natural setting that is most impressive'. Which is as it should be in Iceland.

An hotel and a church; the largest lake in Iceland with two volcanic islands and its own brand of trout called the *murta*; a few dwarf trees, glaciers in the distance, steam rising from a hillside, heather in the autumn, an extinct shield volcano to the north-east. All in colours of ash and sky. Even the river which flows from the southern end of the lake has a bleak name. It is called the *Sog*.

'Leave her to me just for a little while,' I had said. 'I can find out more than you will in a week of interrogation.'

'You're very Goddamn sure of yourself,' Charlie Martz said.

Sigurdson said: 'I think Mr Conran has a way with stewardesses.' He winked to remind me that we had a date before I left to go drinking and find the girls.

'Okay,' Martz said. 'I sure hope you know what you're doing. Jesus Christ' – he explored his cranial stubble – 'she practically blew that poor bastard's head off.'

'She did it for us,' I reminded him.

'Yeah. Like she's been taking messages to London for Christ knows how long and getting this whole Soviet thing set up here.'

Sigurdson shook his head, with admiration almost, and his fringe of pale hair fell across his forehead. 'The trouble is,' he said, 'that we are no nearer the truth. First we had one dead Russian agent – now we have two.'

'We've saved an innocent man from being pilloried,' I said.

Sigurdson didn't reply. I couldn't tell whether he was ruminating on the meaning of pilloried or silently regretting that an American had not been responsible for the girl's death.

I said: 'In any case I don't agree that we're no nearer the truth. Laxdal was the boss – he won't operate any more. You can take his house and office to pieces and you can take Magnusson into custody – meanwhile I'll see what I can get out of the girl.'

'My,' Charlie Martz said, 'you sure pick the tough assignments for yourself.'

So I took Gudrun to Thingvellir, fifty kilometres from Reykjavik, because I had never seen the place and my professional mind thought that the setting and its associations might encourage Gudrun to talk.

I brought a blanket from the car because the lava could be sharp. And a couple of bottles of wine and some loaves and cheese; and a tape-recorder that looked like a transistor radio, and pillows. The air was warm, smelling of mud and moss and honey. I also bought a raincoat and umbrella. As they said, 'Just wait a moment . . .'

First of all she kissed me, which wasn't standard procedure for interrogation. I reached out one hand and switched off the tape-recorder.

After a while she said: 'I am very hungry, Bill.'

The fact that, the day before yesterday, she had killed her former lover, had not markedly affected any of her appetites. She said: 'You are surprised that I am not more in mourning?'

'A little,' I said.

'I am Icelandic,' she said. The phrase which was widely used to explain any strength, weakness or aberration of behaviour. 'If you had read the sagas you would understand the way we are. Besides' – she crumbled a piece of cheese on to a crust of bread – 'I am happy because I am with you and all the badness is over.'

'But I'm afraid it isn't over,' I said. I poured myself a glass of Italian wine and hoped it wasn't an ox-blood and banana-boat vintage.

She held out a glass and said: 'Skal.'

'Skal,' I said. For a moment I could imagine her drinking out of a skull.

She sipped and munched and occasionally stroked me. 'I had a dream last night,' she said after a while.

I poured her more wine and handed her more bread. And, because Icelanders are very fond of recounting their dreams and should, if possible, be deterred, I pointed into the sky. 'Look,' I said. 'Geese. Pink-footed, I think.'

'In this dream you and I were living together in a little white house on the shores of a lake.'

I rose on one elbow. It was ridiculous. 'Gudrun,' I said,

'everything is not over. I want to know everything that happened. From the beginning. When you first became involved with the Communists? How you got to know Laxdal? How long you acted as a courier? Who you had to meet in London?' I gazed across the mauve crust of the earth towards the listening mountains. 'Why you betrayed your country?'

She stopped eating and threw a lump of lava into the lake. The ripples chased each other, gave up. 'I did not betray my country. You must not say that. I did what I thought was best for Iceland.'

'They must have got you very young,' I said.

'Laxdal made love to me when I was seventeen,' she said. 'I was a virgin until then.'

'Great going,' I said.

'That is when a girl should stop being a virgin.'

'And start being a Communist?'

'I want to tell you about this dream. We left the little house and went swimming together in the lake. The water was very cold . . .' She was getting into her stride: it was going to be a saga.

'Gudrun,' I said. 'Forget the dream for now. Tell me how it all began.'

I switched the tape-recorder on again.

She was a student when Protest was just emerging as a force that could no longer be dismissed as youthful frivolity. It still wasn't the ugly phenomenon that it is today; nevertheless the beards and hair were growing and the voice of youth was being heard, angry and strident and usually sincere.

In Iceland, particularly in the winter, Vietnam and anti-apartheid were remote causes. And, with the absence of poverty, dictatorship or Black Power, the potential for protest was meagre. So inevitably Youth turned its attention to the presence of 'The NATO Iceland Defence Force' and the Americans therein.

Equally there wasn't much potential for Communism of the Marxist-Leninist brand. There was little poverty, the standard of living was high and the benefits were shared around – an insurmountable handicap for the revolutionary Communist. So Communism crystallised into indignation over the American presence.

Thus youthful Protest and Communism to an extent mixed. Neither very strong, neither bearing much resemblance to their international brethren on the campus or in the Kremlin. But they elicited some sympathy from a populace which wavered between acceptance of the reality that they needed a defence force and resentment that they had to suffer 'an Army of Occupation'.

Gudrun apparently protested with enthusiasm – her glands didn't permit indifferent participation in anything. But that was all it was: an exuberant intermission in the process of growing up. Until she met Laxdal.

Laxdal, the mercenary of any cause that paid him enough, met her at some sort of political jamboree and discovered that she intended to become an air stewardess. There were no creases then sneaking around his eyes and mouth; he was attractive, virile and mature. He seduced Gudrun – although the verb to seduce has no real place in the Icelandic vocabulary and she thoroughly enjoyed the expert introduction into sex.

Very soon she was in love with him. The sort of love that magazine aunties dismiss as infatuation to be treated on the same level as acne and chafing breasts. Not that they have ever experienced it, of course. With Gudrun the 'infatuation' lasted several years: thus it was love.

She became an air stewardess and had her baby which involved no stigma whatsoever. All the time Laxdal nursed the protest in her soul which had long since been discarded by her contemporaries. And he never stopped talking – in the post-coital sadness perhaps – of his ideals: an Iceland free from foreign occupation.

Then one day he asked her to take some documents to London and pass them over to a Polish friend – Russian probably – in a pub called *The Pheasant* near London Airport. The documents were in a large envelope sealed with wax and addressed to the Secretary of the Freedom For Iceland Society. A society that was more than spurious: it was non-existent. Gudrun agreed because there didn't seem to be any harm in it and it was all connected with Laxdal's ideals; and she was still a Communist of sorts.

Their love continued. Gudrun asked him to leave his wife and he declined. Not everything, after all, was so different in Iceland.

I stopped the tape-recorder for a moment. 'Was there ever a Johann?'

'No,' she said. 'Only Valdimar and now you.' She looked as if she might like to revert to her dream, but I stopped her and switched on the recorder again without her noticing.

She took more documents to London. Presumably details of the progress of Soviet infiltration and the American military set-up. She was the perfect courier: she travelled regularly to London, there was little likelihood of her being suspected, and she didn't ask too many questions. With Gudrun carrying these messages the Russians didn't have to bother about radio messages being monitored or diplomats arousing suspicion by frequent travel.

The Russians had, in fact, assessed her philosophy accurately – the philosophy, possibly, of a few other Icelanders in similar circumstances. She was quite prepared to work for the eviction of the Americans; so were the Russians; it was merely that their motives were different.

Then one day Gudrun grew up – or matured a little. She saw Laxdal out with another girl one evening, attentive and charming. That in itself did not upset her unduly because she knew that he loved only her. Then a couple of nights later she saw him out with his wife, attentive and charming. And in that moment of revelation she saw herself as the other woman. Always the bridesmaid, never the bride.

She told Laxdal that it was all over. She told him that she was bored with carrying mysterious documents to London and that, in any case, his ideals showed no sign of coming to fruition. She also said that she was tired of Communism which wasn't Communism anyway. In effect, she wasn't going to continue with activities that she had performed merely to please her lover.

Her lover had other ideas.

He blackmailed her. He produced photographs of her meeting Russian agents in London and photostats of what he said was one of the documents she had taken to London. The document was a secret report of a Parliamentary sub-committee assessing Icelandic feeling about the presence of the Americans. If she didn't continue to co-operate then he would see that evidence reached the police – after he had left Iceland.

Gudrun debated how to beat the blackmail. And while she was thus engaged a dark stranger entered her life. One, William Conran. She was told he would be on the aircraft, she was told to pick him up, to' become his lover and, if possible, to extract secrets from him in the time-honoured way. A minimum requirement was to supply details of my movements.

'If you wanted to beat the blackmail why the hell didn't you tell me what was going on?' I asked.

'Because they said they would kill you.'

'They'd already tried once,' I said. 'Who was that, by the way?'

'Magnusson,' she said. 'He's a very good shot.'

'Not too good, thank God.'

'I didn't know about the shooting until the other night. Apparently Laxdal got very angry with Magnusson for trying to kill you as soon as you arrived. He said they should wait and see who you were after.'

She gave me a long slow kiss and I switched off the taperecorder again.

Above us a tiny cloud formed in the sky as if it had been generated by the kiss.

I lit a cigarette and gave her one. 'Carry on,' I said. 'Now tell me about the girl who died.'

'I didn't know about that either,' she said. 'I didn't realise that Communism could be so evil.'

'You and a lot of others,' I said.

'Laxdal told me that I was not doing my job properly with you. Be made a hint that if I did not help more then I might die like the girl.'

'That was stupid of him.'

'He was very jealous of you. He did not love me but he was still jealous. He was like that. When he said that about the poor girl I got suspicious. I shouted at him and accused him of killing her. At first he said nothing. Then I said that you were much better than he was in bed.'

I grabbed at the tape-recorder but my alleged prowess was already overheard and noted. And I wasn't in a position to manipulate the eraser.

'That was damned decent of you,' I said in my most English voice.

'I just said it to make him angry,' Gudrun said.

'Thanks,' I said.

'And I succeeded because I knew how conceited he was about the loving.'

'What happened,' I asked, 'on the night the girl died?'

The girl was impressionable. Especially where boys were concerned. Parental control was feeble and she was known to be available at the dances at the Saga and the Loftleidir. There was also some suspicion that she had access to drugs: she certainly had access to liquor through her many boy friends.

She was also Icelandic and therefore intensely patriotic. But it is not difficult to misdirect such loyalties in an impressionable teenage girl who is over-fond of boys and booze. Laxdal, or one of his younger associates, sold the girl the line about getting rid of the American presence. His organisation was, in fact, in the process of manufacturing a series of incidents that would bring American servicemen into disrepute. The girl was to create the first incident.

It was all arranged for the evening when Gudrun and I went to the Saga for dinner. Someone had told Laxdal – one of the youths giving the party, presumably – that Shirey would be there looking for girls. The girl was given several drinks to drown any misgivings she might have and the meeting was set up at the bar.

Her instructions followed classical lines. She was to take him home and encourage him to make love to her. Afterwards she was to tear her clothes a bit and run round to the police alleging assault.

But Laxdal overplayed his hand – a weakness of his. In the first place the girl was given too much to drink; then he became too rough with her when he went round to the apartment and discovered that she had failed to seduce Shirey. Failure in such matters was inexplicable to Laxdal. He told her to tear her clothes and when she was too slow and laborious he lost his temper and slapped her, bruising her mouth.

He realised that she was too drunk to complete her mission and left. By this time she was almost unconscious from the effects of the liquor and the blow on the face. Shortly after Laxdal's departure she vomited and choked to death. Her body was found by an Icelandic youth who had called in the hope of being offered what Shirey had rejected.

'Laxdal admitted it all to me the night I returned from London,' Gudrun said. 'I screamed at him and he slapped me just like he slapped the girl. I was going to tell you because I could not keep the truth from you any longer. But you came back too early. I tried to make you go away again and come back later. But you would not go. I tried to stop you from saying the names of Magnusson and Laxdal. Laxdal would have let you go if he thought you still didn't suspect him. But you had to say them . . .'

She gazed at me fondly, impulsive devil that I was.

I switched off the recorder. I wasn't sure whether she had realised that it was eavesdropping.

About a mile away two men sped past on sturdy little Viking horses – the horses the Norsemen brought with them 1,000 years ago, the horses I rode in my childhood. I felt the saddle again and the flowing movement of muscle as the horses hurried along at the running walk they preferred to trotting.

Overhead some more geese. Grey lags? You couldn't tell at that height. They brought with them loneliness, winter dusks. The sky was paler, the mountains advancing, the sound of water louder. Human intrigue was a mere petulance.

'Time to go,' I said. 'We'll have another session later. Tomorrow perhaps.'

'I don't know anything more,' she said.

'We'll have another session just the same.'

We walked across the ancient ash towards the car. I believed most of what she had said. But it didn't really explain the large sums of money that had been paid into her banking account in the last two or three years – the payments I had been shown by a reluctant bank manager that morning. Perhaps they were to ensure the baby's future.

She threw the two wine bottles behind a crag of lava. I picked them up again and kept them for the car trunk because I didn't like to see the countryside treated like that.

The mallard sat on the grass watching us with benign interest and looking as if it were hatching an egg. Which was all right with me except that it was a male.

The artificial lake in the centre of toytown was torpid and grubby, the nursery houses bright in the evening sunshine.

Jefferey had arranged the *meet* beside the lake. They would always be *meets* with him now – never plain honest-to-goodness meetings. I should have been carrying *The Times* under one arm and wearing a red carnation in my button-hole.

'Well?' I said.

'I was hoping you might have something for me,' he said.

'Such as what?'

'Developments old man. Things seem to have been hopping since our last meeting.'

'Nothing that need concern you,' I said. 'You were rather keen that the British should have nothing to do with the Shirey affair.'

'Don't be so shirty,' he said. 'We thought your intervention was going to be a *faux-pas*. But there's no reason why we shouldn't have a bit of the glory now. British scientist helps to unmask the killer – all that sort of thing.'

I gave the mallard a despairing look. The mallard shifted uneasily on its phantom eggs and looked the other way.

Jefferey said: 'Of course, this doesn't alter anything. The Russians,' – he looked uneasily in the direction of the Soviet Embassy – 'still know who you are and they want you out.'

'Have you heard anything from London?'

'Not yet, old man. After all it was a public holiday yesterday.'

'In Iceland, not in London. You know, you'll have to work

on national holidays if you're going to become a spy, Jefferey.'

He looked as if he would have preferred a stiff upper-cut to stiff upper-lip. He controlled himself and said: 'I think we should give the Press boys a story. After all, it's damned good publicity for the Brits.' He paused. 'And the Americans – after all, we're all in this together.'

'All of us except you,' I said. 'The Americans are handling the publicity on this. Lieutenant-Commander Charles Martz. I believe you've spoken to him on the phone.'

Jefferey said: 'He wasn't very civil.'

'Civil or not, you take your orders from him on this one.'

'Now look here . . .'

'Read this.' I handed him a cable which I had decoded in pencil underneath. 'You'll have to take my word for it because I'm not giving you the cypher.'

The cable from London said: 'Message from embassy says you blown by soviets stop leave developments entirely to your discretion stop replacement will only be sent if you authorise stop you in sole charge in respect NATO mission but presume you will observe diplomatic courtesies stop regards . . .' The cable was signed by someone whose authority was formidable.

I retrieved the cable from Jefferey, rolled it into a ball and considered telling him where he could put it. But that would hardly be a diplomatic courtesy.

Instead I put it back in my pocket. 'I'll eat this later,' I said.

So there we all were together for the first time since my arrival. Charlie Martz, Sigurdson and myself whooping it

up at the Loftleidir. Sigurdson quaffing his asni with enthusiasm and eyeing the considerable talent, Martz and myself
tinkling the rocks in our Scotch and eyeing the talent with
less predatory intent.

The bar was modern, so was the band and the dancing.
The Loftleidir, situated on the city airport, was Reykjavik's
newest hotel – three restaurants, two cocktail lounges,
swimming pool, sauna, floor show, dancing and 'Icelandic
specialities'. Sigurdson made it clear what he considered
the specialities to be.

He was laughing a lot and giving us both friendly punches.
His hair had fallen into its fringe and was more spiky than
usual around the sides. The leader of a spy ring had been
shot dead and he had taken much credit among his own
circles for the shooting: it all compensated for the fact that
an American could not be blamed for the girl's death.

He welcomed his fourth asni with delight while Martz
and myself dawdled along with our second whiskies. Then
he grabbed a large, plump woman and, after informing us
that this was how he liked them, led her on to the floor.
At least you didn't run the risk of a refusal if you didn't
bother to ask a girl if she wanted to dance.

Martz suggested we took our drinks to a corner table
while Sigurdson jogged around with his speciality.

'It's not over yet, Charlie,' I said.

'Don't I know it,' he said. He was more relaxed now that
his liaison duties were less arduous, and I could occasionally
see the gold filling when he grinned.

'How did Shirey take it?'

'He flipped his lid. He said to thank you. That goes for
me too, by the way.' He almost looked embarrassed. 'I've
revised my opinions about you a bit.'

'You should thank Gudrun.'

'Okay, lover,' he said. 'But you know as well as I do that
she'll be charged. Although she might get off fairly lightly

seeing as she did shoot Laxdal. Nevertheless she did take money so it wasn't all youth and naïvety and all that crap.'

'I suppose not,' I said. I studied the ice cubes with their white Christmas trees inside. And to divert my own thoughts from Gudrun I said: 'Where's Shirey now?'

Martz said: 'Back in the United States of America. We flew him out as soon as we knew he was in the clear. It seemed to be the best thing to do.' He beckoned a waiter. 'Shirey was real grateful to you.'

'Thanks for passing on the message Charlie, old buddy,' I said.

Sigurdson returned from the dance floor. But his partner had multiplied – one for each of us. Sigurdson looked proud of himself.

'How are the wife and kids, Einar?' I asked.

'Fine,' he said. 'Just fine.'

The woman who was to be mine said: '*Komid thjer saelir.*' She was a big strong girl with a slight cast in one eye. Martz's partner was small and sulky. They sat down and awaited our pleasure.

'Einar,' I said. 'Not tonight. On the night before I leave, perhaps. But not now.'

Sigurdson offered clumsy understanding. 'You are unhappy about the air stewardess. You need not be. One night with the girl I have chosen for you and you will forget her completely.' The girl he had chosen for me concentrated her gaze on my ear and smiled reassuringly.

Martz said in his appalling Icelandic: 'I am a happily married man with two children.' His girl became sulkier and made up her lips, leaving a smudge of lipstick on her rodent teeth.

'Einar,' I said, 'get rid of them.'

'You do not like? Then I find you others.' He dismissed the two girls like a director auditioning chorus girls.

Martz said: 'Business first, pleasure afterwards, Einar.

Now let's try and work out what we do know. We've pulled both Hafstein's places apart, we've pulled Magnusson's home, apartment and farm apart, we've been over Laxdal's apartment and office and interrogated his widow. We've got practically nowhere. What now?'

'I think Magnusson will break eventually,' Sigurdson said.

'Maybe,' Martz said. 'But we can't rely on it.' He frowned. 'What gets me is that I know we're almost there. I can feel it, Goddamnit. It's the Hafstein angle that's got me beat. Where the hell does he come into it? Everything seems to lead to him – that piece of paper in the dead Russian's pocket. His position in the national register. And now we find papers in Laxdal's safe involving him. Yet he just seemed to be a bird-watching screwball.'

'The implication is noted,' I said.

'You know what I mean. He just wasn't the stuff spies are made of. And now he's dead.'

Sigurdson said: 'Perhaps you would have preferred it if he had shot me.' He laughed into his asni.

'Charlie,' I said, 'isn't it after ten?'

He looked at his big nautical wristwatch. 'Yeah, it's a quarter after. What of it?'

'Shouldn't you be back at base?'

Martz grinned. 'The regulation only says that servicemen have to be off the streets.'

'Then why do the police go round the bars?'

'Just checking up, I guess. After all, if you're in a bar it stands to reason that you'll have to go into the street if you're going to leave.'

A wiry, sallow-faced Icelander came up to the table and showed Martz a plastic-covered card. Behind him stood a square, balding man with a pitted neck. The Icelander said: 'Are you American?'

Sigurdson laughed and sobbed and choked. 'The patrol,'

he managed to say. 'The patrol's come to round up Charlie Martz?'

The American with the pitted neck said: 'What's so funny, wise guy?'

Martz ascertained that he was new to the job, took him aside and told him what was not so funny.

The 11.30 p.m. sun went down and rose again. The light penetrated the curtains with contempt. Outside someone smashed a bottle – I gathered you didn't get your money back on bottles in Iceland.

I closed my eyes and thought: 'German church.' I opened them again and switched on the radio. I picked up the BBC loud and clear. A record programme introduced by a disc jockey with a deep, suave voice. Then a news bulletin including an item about the Soviet naval build-up all over the world's oceans.

I switched off and my thoughts roamed across the city to Gudrun's apartment where she was staying under what amounted to house arrest. I hauled the thoughts back because they had no future.

German church. The two words held the key. What German church? Like Charlie Martz I felt we were almost there. Like Charlie Martz I knew there was something wrong, a barrier of incongruity between us and the truth.

One a.m. – Hafstein, resurrect yourself for five minutes. Bare your soul before me and your birds in their glass cases. Or make the birds speak, for they surely know all the answers. Hafstein, you deceiver of women, you hermit, you idealist, you ornithologist, you madman. The Adam's apple bobbed in the scrawny neck but no words issued forth. Hafstein a spy? Never. And hadn't Laxdal said the same?

I sat upright abruptly. On the table beside the bed were the keys which I had been given if I wanted to stay in the national register after office hours. I hadn't yet checked out the register: that was tomorrow's job. 1.30 a.m. Unquestionably after office hours. But what was conventional time in the Land of the Midnight Sun?

I got up, dressed, and let myself out of the guest-house into the chill, light night.

18

The Files

The national register, the Thjodskrain, is a sub-department of the Icelandic Statistical Bureau which is called the Hagstofa Islands. The bureau produces a catalogue of facts compiled by the Economic Institute. Icelanders drank 0.61 litres of milk per person in 1967; there were 185 cars, 160 TV sets and 330 telephones per 1,000 inhabitants at the end of '68; Iceland has the lowest infant mortality rate in the world.

The Thjodskrain is situated in a building called the Arnarhvoll which houses various other government departments.

I walked through the town centre still wondering why papers involving Hafstein had been found in Laxdal's safe when Laxdal had told me that Hafstein had nothing to do with his organisation. There had been no reason for Laxdal to lie; in fact, he was going to some trouble to find out what I knew about Hafstein when Gudrun shot him.

A policeman nodded at me with the conspiratorial friendliness of those who are abroad while the majority sleep. A group of teenagers occupied a street corner. They were reading a newspaper which extended an apology to the Americans for the injustice of the suspicions that had been aroused: Laxdal seemed to have achieved a considerable improvement in Icelandic-American relations.

I unlocked my way through corridors, offices and cabinets. The atmosphere was as impersonal as the figures in the cabinets; muffled and motionless, smelling occasionally of yesterday's coffee and biscuits and, near the washroom, of sulphur from the water piped from the hot springs.

I let myself into the department where the births, deaths and marriages of Iceland's 200,000 or so people are kept. The pain and jubilation of birth, the courtship and consummation of marriage, the end of the journey – they were all here in flourished, fading ink and uncaring typescript. Unwritten sagas signed, sealed and delivered by shiny fingers in between coffee and lunch breaks.

Conran, I thought, you're getting sentimental – or cynical. The second was only an acknowledgment of the first.

I thumbed through the ledgers until I came to Olav Magnusson. Nothing much there. Born in 1920 – 'muling and puking' and staring at nothing with blue innocent eyes. Or were they innocent? Was not the scheming and the avarice already there inside the soft, unknitted bones of the skull, waiting to develop with all the other faculties? Sentiment and cynicism.

Married twenty-five years ago. Celebrating his silver wedding anniversary in prison awaiting probable charges of treason unless he gave us what we wanted. Then the prospect of a far more savage retribution from his masters than anything the Icelandic courts would ever impose.

No death certificate, Magnusson. Not yet.

Outside, the rasp of an ailing motorcar disturbed the premature day. Then silence, the light waiting for the people. Light with the same texture that first snow gave to the dawns of childhood. Or the light on a honeymoon morning in Switzerland; long before Moscow, long before Iceland.

I found Hafstein's desk and sat down at it. It was as he had left it. A typewriter, a quill pen – there was no escape from his birds – an IN tray and an OUT tray, a blotting pad covered with churches and falcons. Hafstein, what did you know, sitting here bringing statistical order to disordered lives, tugging at that stubborn beard, brooding over the values of your fellows, simplifying justice, exaggerating in justice? What did you know that made you flee to your death?

I waited for the answers but there was no reply. Yet the answer was here somewhere.

I took out Laxdal's documents. Nothing here to indicate a ruthless narcissus. Mother, father, wife. I picked up the documents and imagined I could smell his aftershave; it was the time of day for imaginations to deceive. No death certificate; but that had already been written far away from the pens and typewriters.

Neither Magnusson's nor Laxdal's documents looked like forgeries. You couldn't tell, I knew: that was the idea. But I felt that their papers were genuine. Neither Magnusson nor Laxdal were Russians: they were merely traitors who had enjoyed the money and the secret, gloating self-satisfaction of the spy.

Where, then, were the forgeries? I couldn't sift through a population of *sons* and *dottirs*.

A dog howled in the distance. But there were no dogs in Reykjavik. The dawn deception again. An arrowhead formation of ducks or geese crossed the window, too high up in the grey sky for identification. Hafstein would have had his binoculars out for those.

I sat at the desk waiting. Gradually the sensation that I was being watched embraced me. The sensation, perhaps, that Hafstein had experienced before his flight. I put my hand on the unsentimental butt of the Smith & Wesson that had written Laxdal's death certificate and crossed the room to the door.

With my unarmed hand I pulled the door open and peered at no one. I looked down the corridor but the air and the dust were undisturbed. Just the sound of a tap dripping and the chemistry-set odour of sulphur.

I closed the door and locked it again. The feeling that I was being watched persisted. Like a soldier senses, too late, that he is in a sniper's sights.

From the windows across the way? From binoculars, telescope or telescopic sights? I removed the contents of Hafstein's desk drawer and moved away from the window.

3 a.m. The whine of a jet gathering momentum, the crash of a bottle breaking. Rain against the window.

With the papers from his drawer I once again approached the soul of Hafstein which was, perhaps, resting in peace. Formal letters, bills, catalogues, a sprig of heather that crumbled in my hand, a fragment of lava from Katla perhaps in 1918 or even Hekla in 1947. I knew my lava.

A battered volume by old Snorri Sturluson, a tobacco pouch with a perished rubber lining to which brown flakes still adhered, a metric ruler bearing Hafstein's name in childish writing, a very old cigarette from which the tobacco slid like snuff, a birthday card to Hafstein signed by someone called Petur in 1960. No more birthday cards, Emil, no more cigarettes, no more memories of childhood evoked by the ruler . . .

At the bottom of the pile was a large envelope. Stained, with the flap sealed by time. I slit it open with the schoolboy Hafstein's ruler.

Inside the envelope was an official letter appointing Hafstein to his job in 1942. I sat down among the INs and OUTs, among the typewriters and inkwells, and considered the letters. Instincts, intuitions, memories, promptings, expectations . . . they stirred and shifted like iron filings attracted to a magnet. Why?

It had to be the date. 1942. Why did the date put all senses on alert, engender a state of emergency?

Calm down, Conran. Take it easy, boy. Have a cigarette and contemplate the endless dawn.

I had a cigarette and I contemplated the dawn. I checked the corridor again to see if anyone was listening to my agitation. No one there. I lit another cigarette and tapped the ash in to a waste-paper basket so that I would not give the cleaners too much trouble.

1942. Charlie Martz. Lights and rockets of enlightenment, enough to give a man a coronary. Take it easy, let the thoughts approach the magnet in an orderly fashion.

That was the year the Germans had been infiltrated into Iceland, according to Charlie Martz. But how many of them? Just because some gave themselves up it didn't follow that others hadn't been successfully absorbed into the community. Absorbed into the community – what a phrase! Like a lecturer with a textbook instead of a brain. A textbook on spying. German thoroughness and all that. They, too, must have found a way of cooking the books in the Thjodskrain.

The ash beach of Surtsey. Gunfire and a scientist reaching the body of Emil Hafstein first. 'German church.' There was no bloody German church. Never had been. Hafstein had said: 'German . . . church.' The pause between the unrelated words missed out by the scientist.

I replaced the desiccated past of Emil Hafstein, locked up and ran back to the Chevrolet parked outside the guest-house.

I drove fast, keeping up with my thoughts. The tyres hissed on the wet road and pools of blue sky showed in the watery sky. A coach and some lorries sped towards Reykjavik, the drivers glaring in the way that early-risers – as opposed to all-nighters – do. Behind me two or three cars kept their distance.

Everything was assembling in my mind now, if I could control the speed of my thoughts.

The skies cleared and two Delta Dagger F-102 supersonic interceptors took off from Keflavik. I wondered if there was anything to intercept. "The countryside stretched away in solidified waves and crests, grey-green, black and fawn – apologies for colours.

5 a.m. The earth was steaming lazily on the outskirts of Hveragerdi and a baker was removing black bread from a natural oven in his garden. Fruit grew like wax imitations in the steam-wreathed hothouses. One of them was called Eden.

I drove straight to the pool of boiling mud and the steam jets with the Roman Catholic church 'now disused' perched above. I parked the car on the road and began to climb. Past the grey intestinal mud, past the Japanese gardens of sulphur in the hot steam.

The church was small, a chapel almost. The front and rear were made with pine-wood boards; there was a green door and a wooden cross on the roof. The whole building was supported on either side by mounds of turf four feet wide, and the roof was covered with turf and sword moss. The turf had been recently trimmed – by Hafstein probably.

Fifty feet below the mud bubbled like a stock-pot.

I took out the Smith & Wesson and approached the wooden door with elaborate stealth. Then I kicked it open. Sacrilege. The church felt empty; but you could never tell. It smelled of forgotten worship – a dead fragrance of incense, whitewash and Bibles. Hymns were lodged in the rafters beneath the turf, a psalm or two caught in the fretwork above the altar.

I went in cautiously, still holding the gun, because although the setting was convenient I preferred my own funeral to be Church of England. The silence clothed me like a vestment – as it had someone else recently . . .

The small altar had been devastated, two pews overturned. The stone font had been knocked from its wooden pedestal and cracked, a dozen or so prayer books had been ripped apart, the prayers scattered over floorboards polished by decades of obeisance.

A door leading into a tiny anteroom swung open. But the room was empty.

I picked up one of the pews and sat on it. German . . . church. This was the church. But where was the answer to our prayers?

It didn't look as if my predecessor had found an answer either. The pews had been overturned in thwarted rage, the prayer books ripped up in the last futile formalities of his search.

I swore to myself and apologised to the altar.

There was only one man now who might be able to help – Thorarinsson. Eggert Thorarinsson.

I made a complete search of the church, but I knew as I searched that it was pointless. I closed the door softly and climbed down the cliff to my car. I thought I heard a car start up round the corner, but with the roar of the steam I couldn't be sure. When I reached the Chevrolet there was no other traffic on the road.

I drove into Hveragerdi to see Hafstein's only confidant – the keeper of his hothouse.

It was more of a hut than a house. White walls, red tin roof. Very clean – like Iceland. Steam dribbled from a couple of patches of moist soil in the garden. I imagined Thorarinsson trying to tap someone else's steam like they tapped electricity elsewhere.

I knocked on the door and waited, surveying the hot-houses around. A paradise for small boys with catapults.

After a few minutes a woman came to the door. Middle-aged, elderly – it was difficult to tell; except that she had the illusory girlish air that any woman has when she is disturbed at night with her hair down. But the face beneath the long grey hair was resigned and resentful. If she was Thorarinsson's wife then it was understandable.

'Yes?' she said. She wore a black knitted shawl over a grey nightdress.

'Is your husband in?'

She appraised my suit, my shoes, my shadowed chin – perhaps even the bulge beneath my jacket. 'He's in bed,' she said.

'I won't keep him long. Just a few words. He knows me.' I was almost pleading; you couldn't get tough with little old ladies at 5.15 a.m., however aggressively unpleasant they seemed to be.

'Come back later.' She started to close the door.

'What's the good of that? He'll be gone by then.' I put my new shoe in the door on the assumption that she hadn't the strength to break any bones.

'Haven't you got all you want?'

'Your husband wasn't able to help us very much last time. There are a couple more questions I'd like him to answer.'

She looked at me with hatred. 'I thought you'd hurt him enough already.'

'Hurt him?'

She pulled her shawl tighter around her shoulders. Her hands were swollen with arthritis like her husband's. 'Yes,' she said, 'hurt him.' She pushed the door hard against my foot.

'I don't know what you're talking about.'

From the dusky depths inside Thorarinsson spoke. 'Let

him in. He can't do me much more harm. If you don't, he'll start on you.'

She let go of the door and I went inside. Thorarinsson had propped himself up on pillows. Both eyes were closed between pads of mauve skin, his lips were crusted with dried blood, his nose was out of alignment. One arm was in a sling.

'Who did this?' I asked.

'Who did it?' Three teeth were missing from the front of his mouth. 'Who did this? You know who did it. Your fine friend – that's who did it.'

'Sigurdson?'

He nodded and a drop of blood fell from his mouth, staining the sheet. 'That's his name.' He pointed down at his crotch. 'You should see the rest of my body.'

'I'm sorry,' I said.

At least, I thought, you have had the dubious distinction of being beaten up by a Nazi.

19

Confessional

I sat down in an old leather armchair which wheezed resentfully. First of all I had to know whether Thorarinsson had told Sigurdson what he wanted to know.

Thorarinsson shook his head. 'I told him nothing.'

That seemed doubtful because on the previous occasion Sigurdson's bunched fist had been sufficient to intimidate him. On the other hand there hadn't been much to tell us that time.

I said in Icelandic: 'It didn't take much to make you talk last time.'

He winced. 'I didn't tell you anything that mattered.' His eyes stared at me from between their mauve cushions with loathing. There was also a hint of Icelandic obstinacy there which I hadn't previously noticed.

I said: 'You have to believe me. Sigurdson is not Icelandic – he is German. He was sent here as a boy in the last war. I can help you if you will help me. Otherwise he will return and kill you.'

They looked at me with total disbelief: I couldn't blame them: my mind was only just beginning to accept it.

The woman said: 'How can you expect us to believe this trickery?' She sat on the bedside and looked at her husband with something approaching compassion – perhaps the first kindly emotion that had passed between them for many years.

I lit a cigarette. 'Do one thing for me. Get us all some coffee and I will try and explain.'

'I cannot refuse,' she said.

She went into the kitchen. From his throne of pillows Thorarinsson waited phlegmatically for the questions – or the blows. The room was cramped with ancient furniture which was littered with dusty ornaments and chinaware. There was a bookshelf with a few leatherbound sagas and three snuffboxes on it. Wisps of steam floated past the grimy windows and the gloom was permeated by the smell of sulphur like all of Hveragerdi.

When had I first begun to subconsciously suspect? At the guest-house that night, I supposed. Laxdal had been emphatic that Hafstein had no part in any Soviet plot. Why should he deny it if it were true? So what the hell were documents relating to Hafstein doing in Laxdal's possession? Answer: They had been planted there. Just as Hafstein's name had been planted in the pocket of the Russian agent shot dead in the forest.

The only possible person to have planted the first note was the policeman who shot the agent. Or Einar Sigurdson, *bon viveur*, policeman, spawn of the Third Reich.

Throughout the investigation Sigurdson had exaggerated Hafstein's involvement with a single motive that had nothing whatsoever to do with Russian infiltration. His aim was the elimination of Hafstein in a way that would not arouse suspicion. So, what better way than to create a situation where he was the authorised pursuer and Hafstein was the recognised quarry?

But why, after twenty-eight years, had Sigurdson suddenly

decided to kill the one man who knew the secret of his birth? Hafstein, the young clerk of the Thjodskrain, had obviously known about the insertion of Sigurdson's false documents in 1942. I presumed that in the last mad months of his life he had decided to blackmail Sigurdson. Sigurdson whose whole existence was a deceit; Sigurdson who was therefore a justifiable source of money to finance the publication of his books. I could see Hafstein sitting beside the white church, the wind tugging at his pointed beard, watching a flight of birds in a cold sky, planning revenge on a world in which the values did not correspond to the values that had crystallised in his hermit mind, directing that revenge towards the one man whose fraudulence was vulnerable to his knowledge.

That was why Hafstein had been shot dead on the beach at Surtsey.

The woman returned with a china jug of coffee, hairlined with cracks, and three small cups. We all drank it black because there was no milk or cream. How to convince them?

'Tell me one thing,' I said, 'what was it that Sigurdson wanted to know?'

They looked at me with astonishment. Thorarinsson said: 'You don't know? But you and he are working together.'

'Please believe me,' I said. 'I don't know.'

The woman said: 'It is some sort of trick. Don't tell them, Eggert.'

'Don't worry my dear – I shan't.' He had been brave and he was proud of it.

'Did Sigurdson do that to you in front of your wife?' I asked.

Thorarinsson nodded. Yellow teeth showed between broken lips in what might have been a smile. 'Perhaps that is why I did not tell him anything.'

'I must apologise to you,' I said.

Thorarinsson looked puzzled. 'Why?'

'Because I misjudged you the last time we met.' I went over to the bed and poured him more coffee. The armchair sighed again when I sat down.

Thorarinsson said: 'Hafstein was kind to us.'

His wife said: 'That is why we will not say anything that he would not have wanted us to say.'

'But your husband did tell us what we asked him last time.'

Thorarinsson said: 'Hafstein told me to keep as much secret as possible. But if anyone started to get rough with me to tell them when he left. But that was all I was to tell.' The yellow teeth reappeared. 'I knew that he had gone to the Westman Isles.'

Good on you, I thought. 'Now tell me what it was that Sigurdson was after. It can't do any harm because in any case you think I know.' I lit my third cigarette and drank my second coffee. 'Was it something to do with documents?'

They regarded me with distilled suspicion. 'You really don't know?' Thorarinsson said.

'I really don't. But I think it may have been something concerning documents.' Like Sigurdson's own documents from the Thjodskrain which could be identified as forgeries. 'Did he want to know where Hafstein had hidden certain documents?'

'Yes,' Thorarinsson said. 'That is what he wanted to know.' He asked his wife to bring him a snuffbox. 'How is it that you don't know what your own colleague is looking for?' He took a pinch of snuff clumsily; it was his snuff-taking arm that had been disabled.

'Do you know where those papers are?'

'Why should I tell you? Your colleague beat me up and I didn't tell him.'

'Do you know *what* these documents are?'

'I know nothing about any documents.'

If Hafstein had told him what they were, he would have known that Sigurdson was a German. That at least was the truth. But Thorarinsson did know *where* the papers were. Hafstein had befriended him and he was keeping his pledge. Or did he perhaps think that the envelope containing the documents contained money? Cynicism, the inevitable partner of sentiment.

6 a.m. The village was awakening. Cars, bicycles, children's voices. A bell ringing, glass or china breaking, an angry man's shout.

I said: 'Sigurdson thought the papers were in the disused church near the mud pools.'

Their old eyes looked at me, appraising, giving nothing away.

'If you tell me where the papers are, I will stop Sigurdson returning.'

The woman said: 'Such trickery. It is so obvious, so childish.' She spoke as if I were an erring husband returning from a booze-up with the boys with feeble excuses and a drunkard's breath – as, perhaps, Thorarinsson used to arrive home. She examined her arthritic knuckles.

Thorarinsson took more snuff. 'Yes,' he agreed, 'so obvious.'

'I will pay you for the information.'

Thorarinsson felt his lips, his broken nose, his slit-eyes. 'That's what your friend Sigurdson said. Then he did this. I don't want your money.'

'A lot of money.' Cynicism doing battle once more with sentiment. If only sentiment would win more often.

His wife moved from the bed to a leather chair opposite me. 'How much money?' she said.

Cynicism vanquishing once more. What was a lot of money to them? The equivalent of £100 perhaps. I named a figure in kronur.

Thorarinsson said: 'I don't think we should . . .' He

considered the pride which had withstood the onslaught of Sigurdson's fists and boots. A pride which he had displayed before his wife who was now bargaining for money. What was the point?

She turned on him. 'All our lives we have been without money. Now we have a chance for a little. What good will it do us if you refuse the information? What good will it do you to get beaten up again?' She softened a little. 'You were very brave, my dear. But it is of no use. If this one leaves then the other will return. You will talk eventually – no man can take such beatings without talking. No man of your age. So why should we not have the money?'

The yellow teeth again, a glisten of a smile. 'You thought I was brave?'

She nodded. 'Braver than I ever thought you could be.'

Laxdal had succeeded in improving relations between America and Iceland; now Sigurdson had succeeded in bringing a modicum of understanding to an old couple who had hitherto shared only antagonism. And perhaps some cash to go with it.

I said: 'So you do know where these papers are.'

'We might,' he said, with farcical evasiveness.

His wife said: 'But the money you offer is not enough.'

'How much did Sigurdson offer?'

'Much less. An insult.'

I believed her. Niggardly souls often existed beneath brash exteriors. But how much of the brashness was assumed? An Icelandic exterior wrapped round a Nazi core – a formidable combination.

I grinned suddenly and named the equivalent of £500.

Her lips munched greedily around her gums. 'Why do you laugh?'

Because I envisaged London ordering Jefferey to pay her. But I couldn't explain that. 'Because I would like to give you the money.'

Thorarinsson said: 'Because it is not your money to give, I think.'

'Perhaps.'

His wife said: 'But that is not enough.'

'I can't offer more.'

She shook her head impatiently as if no larger sum of money existed. 'I do not mean that. I mean that we must have our safety guaranteed.'

'I will do that,' I said. 'There is only Sigurdson who can harm you and I will take care of him.'

Thorarinsson paused in the act of taking snuff. 'But you two are together. How can we believe that?'

To hell with you, I thought. You're getting £500. No more bargaining. Not even if you were both centenarians. I summarised the situation with Sigurdson and said: 'I'm not offering any more money. If you take it and tell me where the documents are then I give you my word that Sigurdson will not harm you. If you don't then I cannot guarantee that Sigurdson will not return and finish the work he started.' I paused. 'When did Sigurdson do this, by the way?'

'On our National day,' Thorarinsson said.

The day after he had shot Hafstein. Because for Sigurdson there had never been any mystery about 'German Church'. He was the German and there was only one obvious church.

The woman spoke, her voice hoarse with avarice. 'How can we be sure that you will give us the money?'

'You can't,' I said. 'But I'll write out something promising you the money. That's the best I can do. You also have my word.'

She massaged her knuckles; one of them made a noise like a peapod splitting. 'Very well,' she said, 'we will trust you. There is nothing else we can do.'

Thorarinsson made one last show of defiance. 'Perhaps we shouldn't . . . I promised Hafstein.'

'He's dead,' his wife said. 'And so will you be if Sigurdson returns.'

It was the end of his resistance. He took more snuff, his bruised head fell back in the pillows.

I wrote out a promissory note. She took it, examined it, almost sniffed it, and stuffed it down the front of her night-gown.

'And now,' I said, 'where are those documents?'

Another glisten of yellow teeth. 'In the church,' he said. 'Just like Hafstein said as he died. He wanted that scientist to know so that he would tell the police. The real police . . .'

'But Sigurdson turned the place inside out before he came here.'

The yellow teeth disappeared. The joke was over, the whole act was over. He put a weary hand to his forehead. 'In the confessional. Under one of the floorboards.'

'Thanks,' I said. 'There's just one thing . . .'

He didn't reply.

'Why did you refuse to tell Sigurdson?' I hoped it was because of his promise to Hafstein, not because he thought there was money beneath the confessional floorboards.

'Because Hafstein told me not to. I kept my promise.'

And who could dispute it? They would get their equiv-alent of £500 and live a little more happily ever after. Neither sentiment nor cynicism had triumphed.

Before returning to the church I stopped at the Eden hothouse and gave Charlie Martz a call.

I took a wrench from the boot of the Chevrolet and climbed the cliff to the church. Steam hissed high into the air from the level of the mud pools and a breeze blew it around the church.

I left the door open to give me some light. Then I went into the confessional and knelt, but not to confess. I jammed the wrench under one board and prised it open. Nothing.

Tendrils of steam wandered past down the aisle towards the altar. I dug the wrench down again. 'Three Hail Mary's, my child.' Nothing.

I squatted there for a moment, sweat cold on my forehead. Then dug down again, wrench splintering the yellow pine-wood. 'Two Stations of the Cross, my child.'

I slid my hand under the remaining boards and found the envelope. The voice from the other side of the grill said: 'I'll have that, please.'

Sigurdson added in a conversational tone: 'I can see you quite well so don't try anything. And, of course, the woodwork won't stop a bullet.'

I stayed kneeling, envelope in hand. 'I have a feeling,' I said, 'that it's you who should be kneeling. And confessing.'

'Perhaps you are right.' He laughed but the laugh tailed away. 'On the other hand, perhaps my only crime was to be very young during the last war.'

'I don't think that was your only crime.'

'Ah, you mean the killing of Hafstein? That had to be done. He was a dirty blackmailer anyway.'

'And the beating-up of Thorarinsson.'

'He will live,' Sigurdson said.

But Thorarinsson wouldn't live if I allowed Sigurdson to escape. Because, with me dead, Thorarinsson would be the last person alive who could incriminate Sigurdson. And Thorarinsson's wife.

'Let us go where we will be more comfortable,' Sigurdson said. 'Out there on the pews. Stand up, throw your gun away, put your hands behind your neck and walk very slowly down the aisle. My gun is following you.'

I sat in front of the nave and he pulled up one of the overturned pews so that we faced each other.

'The envelope,' he said.

I handed it to him. He checked the papers inside and

relaxed a little. 'Forgeries,' he said. 'But very good ones. We Germans are very thorough. '

'Heil Hitler,' I said. 'How did you find me here?'

'I have had you followed nearly all the time. When you went to the Thjodskrain and then dashed up here I knew that you must have realised the truth. But you left the church empty-handed. So I knew that you had been as unsuccessful as me. However, the envelope was in the church somewhere – I knew that. So I waited here to see if you could persuade Thorarinsson to tell the truth.' He grinned. 'Your powers of persuasion are greater than mine. How much did you pay him?'

'Nothing,' I lied, defending sentiment.

'I do not believe you. However, it does not matter. I shall have to kill you and that will be a pity because I have enjoyed working with you. The Icelander and the Englishman.'

'The German and the Englishman,' I said.

'No,' he said emphatically, and the curtain of hair fell across his forehead. His thick face was tired, his jowls were thick with pale stubble. 'I am an Icelander. Ever since I was a child I have been one. That is the way I want to stay – with my Icelandic wife and my Icelandic children. The accident of birth is forgotten. I am proud to be an Icelander.'

'I shouldn't think they'd be very proud to have you if they knew the truth,' I said. 'Why didn't you give yourself up or get caught like the others?'

He shrugged, resting the gun, a Luger, on his knee. He was flanked by the pulpit; behind him was the altar made of varnished wood, fretted with ornate scrolls and cornices. Sulphury steam wandered around the nave – incense distributed by a phantom priest.

'All the others ended up in captivity,' I said. 'Why not you?'

'My father was captured. We were landed together by a U-boat. We were supposed to head for a farmhouse where we were expected. But the police and the Americans caught my father in a village. I was down the street but no one took any notice of me because no one expected German children to be landed.' He reached for cigarettes with one hand and threw me one. 'Like the Russians, we Germans thought ahead. I could even speak Icelandic – like other children who were being trained could speak Norwegian or French. Or English.'

He leaned over and lit my cigarette with his lighter.

I said: 'What did you do when your father was captured?'

'I hid. I had instructions about what to do if he did get caught. You know, Germany was very eager to get a foothold in Iceland. Like the Russians, she knew it was the key to the North Atlantic.'

'Like the British and the Americans,' I said.

'Sure, like the British and Americans. Even before the war we were trying to get Lufthansa installed here.'

'We?'

'The Germans.'

'I thought you said you were Icelandic.'

'I am now. I think I only stayed German for two years perhaps. My father was captured, my mother died in the air raids on Berlin. I had no brothers or sisters.'

'Did you go to the farmhouse?'

He inhaled deeply and aimed a jet of smoke at a nomadic curl of steam. 'I did. Most of the Icelanders who had been persuaded by the Germans to take in spies gave their "guests" up to the police almost immediately. But not my foster parents. Because I was a child, I suppose, and they had none of their own.'

'It's very touching,' I said.

'They were very good to me. And they didn't regard themselves as traitors. The British invaders or the American occupiers were just as much enemies as the Germans. They were paid, of course – just like Hafstein.'

'Yes,' I said. 'Tell me about Hafstein.'

Sigurdson picked up the envelope lying on the floor. 'There's not much to tell. It was he who planted these papers in 1942 when he was a very junior clerk. For years he kept silent about it. Then he went a little mad and started to blackmail me.'

'But what about your father's papers? When the police checked those out they must have found that they were phoney. Why didn't they find yours as well?'

'Because the Germans had anticipated that if one of us was caught the documents would give the other one away. So my father was given a different name altogether. Möller, I believe.'

'So you grew up like a good little Icelander?'

'Or a bad little Icelander.' Sigurdson laughed hugely. 'Always I like the girls and the drink.'

'Even when you were ten?'

Sigurdson considered his precociousness. 'Not at ten, perhaps. But at twelve I liked the girls.'

'The Germans chose well,' I said. 'You seem to have been more Icelandic than the Icelanders.'

'Or perhaps it was my environs.'

'Environment,' I said.

'Yes, perhaps that's what it was. Perhaps we grow up like our surroundings, not like our parents so much. Certainly all the boys where I was brought up in the north liked the girls very much.'

I measured the distance between Sigurdson and myself. A kick would reach the Luger. But Sigurdson was too astute for that. I wondered where he planned to kill me.

'Why didn't you get hold of the forged papers before? After all, you were a policeman.'

'Why should I? The papers said that I was an Icelander

by birth. Why should I want to remove such fine proof of my birth?' Sigurdson squashed his cigarette stub and fondled the barrel of the Luger with his free hand. 'Then Hafstein went crazy and started demanding money to publish these absurd books of his. I knew then that I had to kill him because you never bargain with a blackmailer. I gave him some money to shut him up and thought about the best way to dispose of him. It was just about the same time that Martz and I were getting worried about the Russians.'

'Were *you* really worried? '

Sigurdson looked hurt. 'Of course I was worried. This is my country.' He grinned again. 'And in any case, even if you dispute my Icelandic nationality, I was born in a Fascist state which did not appreciate Communism very much.'

And you still look like a German, I thought. Given different clothes, a slicker haircut, the relaxed figure that beer and cream cakes gives to Burgomasters. Holidaying in the Tyrol, slapping leather-covered thighs and denouncing the Gestapo past. Certainly Sigurdson had retained some of the characteristics which conception in Nazi Germany had impregnated in his soul. The easy conscience about killing and brutality. A middle-aged Hitler youth.

'You were so worried,' I said, 'that you put your future comfort before the interests of Iceland. You deliberately sabotaged our efforts to break the Soviet ring so that Einar Sigurdson could live happily ever after with his wife and kids.' Somehow I had to keep Sigurdson talking in the hope that Charlie Martz was on his way.

'You are wrong, my friend.'

'I'm not bloody wrong.'

A car passed along the road beneath. The door of the anteroom moved in the breeze blowing in through the open door. The breeze chilled me and accentuated the imminence of death. I shivered and thought of nursery gardens, girls like *Alice in Wonderland*, of my first car, my first job and all that might have been.

Sigurdson said: 'You are wrong. In the first place Laxdal is dead and Magnusson is in captivity. I found a list of names and places in Laxdal's possession. We will round them up later. Unhappily, my friend, you will not be here to see that.'

'Why didn't you release the names before?'

'Because I wanted to clear this mess up once and for all and convince everyone that Hafstein was a spy. You, Mr Conran, kept throwing doubt on that. It was most distressing. So I planted false documents about him in Laxdal's apartment.'

'Just as you planted Hafstein's name in the Russian spy's pocket in the forest?'

'So you knew that?'

'I guessed it,' I said. 'Too late. Once suspicion was directed against Hafstein it was easy for you to prepare a false dossier on him. Then rig a chase and kill him. How did you make him run for it?'

'As you said, it was easy. Too bloody easy.' He tasted the phrase. 'You know I like your word *bloody*. The Americans do not use it too much.'

'It's a good word,' I said.

'Too bloody easy. Yes, that's what it was. I just told him that the Americans and British – Martz and you – suspected him of being a Russian spy. I said that if you questioned him it would only be a matter of time before he told the truth – no one can stand up to expert interrogation.'

'Some innocent old men seem to manage it,' I said.

He ignored me; perhaps because the Nazi in him saw no harm in beating up old men. He went on: 'I advised him that if he told the truth I would be blown – is that how you say it? Blown?'

'Some of us do,' I said.

'And if I was blown, he would not get any more money. I advised him to get out of the way. Fly to the Westman Islands where I knew he sometimes used to escape from life in a cave up the cliffs. I even gave him a gun.'

'Then you planned to follow him and kill him *in the pursuit of your duty*?'

'That's right,' Sigurdson said. He beamed. The breeze was becoming colder; or perhaps death was approaching closer.

'But things weren't quite so easy then, were they Sigurdson? You didn't know – or had forgotten – that Hafstein had one friend in the Westman Islands. She heard that you were flying across officially to capture Hafstein and warned him. It was then that Hafstein realised he had been double-crossed. That you were coming to kill him. That was it, wasn't it, Sigurdson?'

'That was it.' He stretched, relaxed; muscular and lethal. 'But as you know I found out from the cave where he was running to. So I followed and got the first shot in, just in case Hafstein decided to give himself up to any scientists who might have been around. But then I found that Hafstein had double-crossed me. He had taken my documents from the Thjodskrain but he hadn't brought them with him as I had instructed him. Of course to me "German . . . church" meant only one thing. He was trying to tell the scientist that I was a German and that the documents were in a church. This church.' He sighed. 'But I couldn't find the bloody things.'

'Bloody bad luck,' I said.

'It has all come all right in the end.' He gave me another cigarette and lit it. 'Your last I'm afraid.'

'How are you going to explain my disappearance?'

'I shan't,' he said. 'Why should I? People disappear in Iceland on the glaciers, in the mountains, down the volcanoes, in the mud pools . . .' His tongue played with the last two words and I knew my intended destination. 'I am above suspicion. I shall organise search parties for you. Co-operate with my good friend Commander Martz. Soothe the distraught air-stewardess. Then after a few days I shall *find* the list of agents and addresses and we shall round them up.'

'And what of Thorarinsson and his wife?'

'I shall have to kill them. But they are old. They wouldn't know how to spend the money that you have given them.'

'How will you explain their deaths?'

'It doesn't really matter. A fire, perhaps. An accident, natural causes, call it what you will. They will be dead and that's all there will be to it.' He stamped on his cigarette. 'And now we must go. Even the son of a Nazi does not like to kill in a church.' His grip tightened on the butt of the Luger. 'You know,' he said, 'I shall always regret that we did not go out together and find some girls.'

I crashed my first car, forgave my wife, forgave the Russian girl, loved Gudrun, remembered parents long-since dead, winked over Sigurdson's shoulder and kicked at the Luger with my right foot.

Sigurdson leaped back knocking the pew over. My foot missed and he fired. The bullet hit me in the thigh – the same leg that I had injured on the cliffs. It slammed me back against the pew and I thought for a moment that the femur had been shattered. But it was only a flesh wound. There was no pain: only shock and blood trickling off the shiny seat and splashing on the floor. A curl of blue smoke from the Luger joined an inquisitive cloud of steam from the doorway.

Sigurdson said: 'Not quite fast enough, my friend.'

I agreed that it wasn't.

'Now we have spilled blood in a church,' he said.

'I don't recall such niceties ever bothering the Nazis.'

'I am not a Nazi. I am not even a German – I am an Icelander.' He looked at my leg solicitously. 'This is very messy. I wanted you to die cleanly. It was the least I could do for you.'

'Thanks,' I said. The pain was beginning, an aching protest from butchered tissue. I was glad the femur wasn't broken: I didn't want to die with a broken femur.

Sigurdson stepped back on to the altar steps. 'I shall have to clean the blood up,' he said.

'I wish I could help you,' I said. Death approached even closer, stepped precisely over the splashes of blood and sat beside me on the pew. The cold filled my body and soul: there was nothing more to do – I had said my last farewells.

'I am glad you tried to outwit me,' Sigurdson said. 'I expected it of you.'

'I'm glad I didn't let you down.'

The grin reappeared: he was his old self again. 'Now we will go to the entrance of the church. Then we will have to say goodbye.'

I stood up and tried my accident-prone leg. It felt sick, as if it wanted to faint all on its own. But it took my weight with help from the pews. I felt as if life were leaving my body before Sigurdson fired the executioner's shot.

We were about half way down the aisle when I felt the thudding underground. As if we were standing on a drum and someone was thumping the skin from the inside. I knew what was happening; I wasn't sure whether Sigurdson did; although he was an *Icelander*.

He jammed the Luger in my spine. 'Faster,' he said. There was urgency in his voice, possibly fear. He knew what the thuds meant: they were the classic prelude to a geyser sprouting. It bad probably been imminent – but aggravated by the shot.

I did my best not to hurry and waited for Sigurdson's last shot. It came as we reached the font. But the bullet smashed into the roof, its impact and the detonation from the Luger lost in primeval noise.

As Sigurdson pulled the trigger the floor tilted and the earth roared. The altar crashed forward, one wall swung outwards as if it were on hinges, the floor split open. Through the gaping wound in the boards I glimpsed water, steam, smoke.

The building tipped forward towards the cliffs. Sigurdson was coming at me, trying to keep his balance, waving the gun high in the air. I tried to steady myself and chopped at his throat with the side of my hand. It hit him below the ear. But it seemed irrelevant . . . the chasm split wider as if giant sutures had been removed and the earth roared again in pain.

The pews slid across the floor, one slamming into Sigurdson's back. He fell towards me, dropping the Luger. I picked it up and ran outside, the weakness in my leg forgotten.

The church was on the edge of the activity. A hundred yards away a dome of water rose slowly, a great shining bubble inflated from the centre of the earth. I scrambled for the cliff, taking my leg with me. Behind me the church tipped sideways as the wound in the earth widened. Sigurdson tumbled out of the porch and started after me.

The dome of water lingered as if there were subterranean observers inside. Then sighed and subsided. I took a shot at Sigurdson with his own gun – a pygmy weapon in these surroundings. The bullet missed and sang around the lava rocks. Sigurdson didn't bother to take cover. He just came on, attacking, Germanic, inexorable.

The ground was shuddering and there was thunder beneath us. Another bell of water rose, lingered and subsided. Vaguely I remembered the text-book description of the birth of a geyser. It would happen now . . .

The second dome of water was followed by a roar of escaping steam. Fifty, sixty, a hundred feet high. As if it had been imprisoned since the beginning of time. High above the jet an umbrella of cloud – like man's imitative penumbra. The heat intensified, the ground moved.

I stumbled down to the rocks beside the pool of boiling mud and waited for Sigurdson behind a crag of moss-covered lava. But I had forgotten that he had my Smith & Wesson. The bullet buried itself in the soft rock beside my head with a thick impact.

I shot back. He was crouching behind another rock. Another bullet embedded itself in the lava beside me. Steam from the springs and steam from the geyser floated in between us. The new jet roared and the earth moved again.

Blood flowed from my thigh, the sick weakness returned. I was aware of my puniness, crouched there on the wafer crust of the world. I felt as if I could poke a hole in it with my finger. Weakness, dizziness, outlines of mountains and the fallen church wavering, the gun heavy in my hand. Icy sweat slid into my mouth.

The earth moved again, settling itself for the last time. Fifty yards away where Sigurdson was crouching the ground cracked open. Sigurdson leapt for his life and met death.

As he leapt I fired. The bullet hit him in mid-air and punched him sideways. He screamed briefly. Landed on the edge of the mud pool, staggered, grabbed at nothing, and fell in.

I dragged myself towards the pool. Just his head, shoulders and chest. The fringe across his forehead, his mouth wide open. His eyes seemed to be looking at me but I couldn't be sure. I hoped he was dead. Now just his head and shoulders. Then the final swallow.

The grey mud belched and I passed out.

20

Black Death

I rather hoped the limp endowed me with a new romanticism. Like the old theory of the man at a party with a black patch over his eye. Didn't the girls ever realise that it only covered a sty?

Charlie Martz didn't think the limp looked romantic. 'Bill, you old son of a gun,' he said, 'you look as if you've got gout.'

'Thanks,' I said.

'Coffee?' he asked.

'On you?'

'Sure.'

I bought a copy of *Morganbladid*. Hekla was still erupting; there was also a paragraph about the new geyser near Hveragardi.

There was ten minutes till my London-bound Boeing took off.

Martz toasted me in coffee. 'Look at those guys over there,' he said.

The two Russian diplomats stood stiff and dour beside the gift counter as if they were wearing cement jackets under their raincoats.

Martz said: 'They're either going to London to be executed or they're waiting to meet the next batch of spies. They sure need some replacements.' The gold tooth glinted in the back of his big laughing mouth.

'Are you sure you got them all?'

He shrugged. 'As sure as I can be of anything. Sigurdson had the list all right. And, as you know, Magnusson confirmed it.' He poured more coffee. 'I wonder what the Soviets make of Communism Icelandic style.'

'They'll carry on trying to change it,' I said. 'They won't give up. One of these days I'll be back to get you out of a mess again.'

'I'll look forward to that,' Charlie Martz said. 'Let's hope that I'll still be around to rescue you when you've got yourself shot and to stop you from bleeding to death.'

'What about the girl?' I asked.

'She might get off with two years. You never can tell with the courts here. They don't really know what to do with criminals, let alone beautiful spies. But you'll be back . . .'

'Maybe,' I said.

A woman's voice called the flight in English and Icelandic. We shook hands, very hard, and grinned at each other.

The two Russians didn't move.

'They're waiting for new recruits,' I said. 'They're your pigeons, Charlie. Better get a tail on to them now. It's all just beginning again.'

'Pigeons,' he said. 'Once a bird watcher, always a Goddamn bird watcher.' He turned and walked out of the civilian building towards his headquarters at the NATO Icelandic Defence Force.

Far below, Iceland slipped away. Black, brown and mint-sauce green. The Ice Age melted in the south by the Gulf Stream. The key to the North Atlantic. The tip of the volcano that was the world.

There was only the metallic sea beneath us when I smelled her perfume. And from the corner of my eye saw the blue blouse and soft blonde hair.

'Would you like a drink, sir?'

I looked up into the blue eyes of a stranger.

'Yes please,' I said. 'Do you have a Black Death?'

Also available

The Twisted Wire

Richard Falkirk

The 1970s Middle East conflict is the setting for this high-octane thriller by the author of *The Chill Factor*.

A crossed telephone wire causes a call from the President of the United States to his Ambassador in London to be overheard by geologist Tom Bartlett. Tom, preoccupied with thoughts of the conference he is to attend in Israel, puts the incident from his mind, unaware that he might not have been the only person listening in . . .

He has not been in Tel Aviv a day, however, before the first attempt is made on his life. As Arab, Israeli, Russian and American agents begin to converge on him, it's clear that someone wants Tom's briefcase – and will stop at nothing to obtain it.

'Unflagging action and good writing.'

NEW YORK TIMES

Also available

The Gate of the Sun

Derek Lambert

On the bitter battlefields of the Spanish Civil War, an unlikely friendship is forged. Tom, an idealistic American, and Adam, a wayward young Englishman, fight on opposing sides, yet they have one thing in common – a passionate love for Spain . . .

With a fervour to match their own, a woman of Madrid is battling in the same bloody struggle. She is Ana, the Black Widow; young, beautiful, bereaved – and a dangerous freedom fighter.

But the end of the armed conflict will not end the conflicting emotions that draw these people together. For over forty turbulent years, from the dark days of Franco's victory to the birth of modern Spain, they will be bound together in an intricate web – of love, betrayal, ambition and revenge . . .

'Gripping . . . a cross between Harold Robbins and Hemingway.'

SUNDAY EXPRESS